GATE CRASHERS

Jules and Yvette ran the last hundred meters of the corridor and stopped. In front of them was the wide wooden door that led to command central. Three guards stood in front of it. Two more stood in blaster-proof booths on either side of it.

"We could cut down the three at the door," whispered Yvette, "but the two in the booths are going to be a problem."

"Let's go back to the car," Jules responded. "I've got an idea."

They jogged back to their vehicle and got in. Jules backed the car half a kilometer down the corridor, then gunned it forward with full acceleration. In seconds, they saw the door rushing up to meet them at a speed in excess of 150 kilometers per hour.

"Hold on tight!" shouted Jules, as the car rammed full tilt into its target. . . .

*Other books in this exciting new series
created by E. E. "Doc" Smith*

Look for new volumes in
THE FAMILY D'ALEMBERT SERIES

GETAWAY WORLD

E. E. "DOC" SMITH

with

STEPHEN GOLDIN

PYRAMID BOOKS ▲ NEW YORK

GETAWAY WORLD

A PYRAMID BOOK

Copyright © 1977 by Verna Smith Trestrail

Pyramid edition published May 1977

Library of Congress Catalog Card Number: 77-73693

Printed in the United States of America

Pyramid Books are published by Pyramid Publications (Harcourt Brace Jovanovich, Inc). Its trademarks, consisting of the
word "Pyramid" and the portrayal of a pyramid, are registered
in the United States Patent Office.

Pyramid Publications
(Harcourt Brace Jovanovich, Inc.)
757 Third Avenue, New York, N.Y. 10017

dedicated to my father and stepmother, David & Ann
Goldin . . . for all the right reasons.

—S. G.

CHAPTER 1

A Chat with Lady A

The young woman looked vastly out of place standing in the line of people waiting to file through the debarkation gate and receive billeting assignments. Tall and lithe, beautiful and dignified, she looked like a tulip growing in a cactus garden. The rest of her queuemates were the scum of a dozen worlds; virtually all of them, male and female alike, were graduates of the roughest schools in the Galaxy—the imperial prison system. They were tough and, for the most part, ill educated; one could tell their planets of origin by the brand of slang they spoke and the choice of obscenities with which they peppered their conversation.

In contrast, the young woman was striking in her cleanliness. Her clothing fitted her with fidelity, and had been fashioned by one of Earth's finest designers. Her eyes had a deep look of intelligence to them, and her long black hair was neatly trimmed. Her stance, the way she tilted her head, the expression of cool self-assurance—all testified to the fact that this woman was something special, born to wealth if not to the nobility itself.

She stood patiently in the corridor that had once been painted white, but was now scratched and faded to a dismal shade of gray. Her eyes stared straight ahead at the tables where the computer programmers were feeding the information on people's cards into their quietly humming machines. She seemed totally unaware of the lecherous glances from the men around her, or of the envious stares from the women. When the person at the front of the line was finished, she moved forward with the rest; but as for any other interaction with her queuemates, she might as well have been a statue.

Finally her turn came. She handed over her cards to the woman at the front table, who took them routinely without looking up and began typing them into the computer. "Name?" the clerk asked in a bored tone.

"Hazel Whiting," the young lady replied. "It's on the card, if you'd bother to look."

The cultured timbre of that voice made the clerk look up. She was obviously startled; she wasn't used to seeing people of such obvious quality in *this* place. "What's someone like you doing here?" she asked involuntarily.

"The same as everyone else—looking for sanctuary."

The clerk was doubtful. This young lady looked too clean, too innocent and too intelligent to be needing this planet's specialized services. Her left foot reached out and pushed the hidden button that would notify the boss that something was not quite right here; the trivision cameras in the corners would beam the scene to his office, where he could make a decision without the applicant's being aware of it. In the meantime, the clerk would carry on with her work. "What did you ever do to need sanctuary?"

"Again, it's on the card," said the woman who called herself Hazel Whiting. "Jewel robberies, mostly, with a few swindles along the way." She paused, then added as a sarcastic afterthought, "It *helps* to look sophisticated; it gets you into the swanker circles where the real loot is."

The clerk shrugged and continued typing silently for several seconds. Then she produced a retinascope, and Hazel Whiting leaned forward to have her identity

8

checked. When the clerk was satisfied, she handed Gospozha Whiting a plastic key card, a pamphlet and a bookreel. "You'll live solely on your past earnings as long as you're on Sanctuary," she said routinely. It was clearly a speech she'd made many times before. "We don't steal from each other here. Report to Room J-5 down the hall for temporary quarters until you decide where in the city you want to live."

Hazel Whiting took the proffered materials from the clerk and started away. As she moved past the line, one of the men grabbed her arm. "Hey, Hazel Whiting," he said in a raspy voice. "How'd you like to move in with me when you get the chance?"

The girl looked him up and down skeptically. The man was a burly sort with more muscle than brains; he smelled as though he'd missed his bath three months in a row, and his beard looked to have been trimmed with pinking shears. "I think," she replied coolly, "I'd prefer to drink vacuum through a short straw."

The man gave a coarse laugh and pulled her closer to him. "I'll teach you not to be so damned snooty."

Hazel Whiting let herself be pulled until she stood right next to the man. Then, in a series of rapid movements, she acted. Her left foot came down hard on her assailant's right instep, causing him to howl with pain and let go of her right arm. Her right hand lashed out, fingers stiff and extended, and jabbed the man just under his ribs. It could have been a killing blow if she had chosen, but that was not her intention. The man doubled over far enough for her to lift her right knee and hit him on the chin with it. He went out like a candle in a gale.

To an accompaniment of whistles and cheers from other men in the line, Hazel Whiting walked off to Room J-5 to obtain her temporary billeting assignment.

Garst was understandably nervous. Seated across from him was the woman he knew only as Lady A, the person most responsible for his being in this position right now. She was easily the most beautiful woman he'd ever seen; the lines of her face had the classic arrangement of eternal beauty. Her creamy complexion was flawless and her calm green eyes took in everything worth seeing in the room. Her body was sensuality incarnate, and her delicate perfume exuded femininity. There was an eternal quality about her. She could have been any age between thirty and sixty; it was impossible to tell, and Garst did not dare ask.

She was dressed in a wide-sleeved panné velvet jumpsuit with flared pant legs. The suit was green, diagonally slashed with black—the left leg and sleeve were black, with thin lines of emeralds along the edges. A tight green hood—attached to the jumpsuit by a gold metal collar—covered most of her jet black hair. A pearl dangled over her forehead from the center of the hood and around her neck she wore an integrated circuit chip on a golden chain.

Yet despite her physical perfection, there was a coldness emanating from her that made her seem terribly inhuman. Her manner was brisk, her speech sarcastic and stern. Garst could not recall ever having seen her laugh in the several months of their acquaintance. It was as though, being possessed of an ideal body, she had relinquished the option on her soul.

Lady A sat in the comfortable chair across from his desk, her right leg crossed over her left and her hands folded neatly into her lap. She stared with piercing intensity at Garst as she spoke.

"I'm very happy with the operation as you've redefined it," she said. "In only slightly over three months you've taken a marginally working system and turned it into a full-fledged organization. Our 'colony' is growing

10

by leaps and bounds; we should soon have enough talent here to launch our recruiting drive effectively."

Garst nodded his head in acknowledgment of the praise. Though Lady A's words were laudatory, her tone of voice had not altered perceptibly; she was still as passionless as an asteroid. "Thank you. As I told you at our first meeting, organization is my forte. The system I had built on Vesa worked perfectly for two decades before bad luck destroyed it last year—and that was working almost entirely on my own. With your backing, there should be no limit to the things I can accomplish."

He leaned back in his chair, daring to relax a little. "In fact," he continued, half joking, "with my talents and your connections, I wouldn't be surprised if the two of us were ruling the Empire within a couple of years."

The woman snorted. "I doubt it. That particular plum has been within my reach before, but it's a harder fruit to pick than it appears. We'll need a little more time and a lot more background work completed before that goal is attained."

Garst did his best not to overreact to Lady A's statement. His own remark had been intended in jest; her answer was dead serious. She did have her eyes set on the Throne; but what did she mean that it had been within her reach before?

A light began flashing on his desk, startling him out of this reverie. Lady A noticed it, too. "What's that about?" she asked.

Garst reached across the desktop and punched some computer key buttons. "It's a signal from Admissions," he announced after a moment.

"Trouble?"

"Probably nothing. We're just having a new shipload coming in today, and I usually get at least one checkup per ship. I've left standing orders that anything in the

11

least bit suspicious is to be referred to me, so that I can make a decision personally. I like to keep on top of my entire organization—it's what makes me so successful." He neglected to add that, since the breakup of his robbery and murder ring on Vesa, he was extremely paranoid about detection. He wanted to stop problems *before* they had a chance to start.

Flipping a couple more switches, Garst turned on the monitors so that he could view the scene at the admitting gate. Out of courtesy to his visitor, he swiveled the set around so that she could see, too.

Both of them watched and listened in silence as Hazel Whiting had her interview with the clerk. They noted the brief but vicious fight in the line with the overzealous male, and Garst gave a low whistle of appreciation at the woman's talent for self-defense. "That Hazel Whiting can certainly handle herself well," he said as the subject moved down the corridor and out of the camera's view.

"That she can," acknowledged Lady A icily. "Except her name is not Hazel Whiting—it's Helena von Wilmenhorst."

There was a pause as she let Garst digest that morsel. "Any relation to the Grand Duke?" he asked at last.

"Only his daughter," replied Lady A from the heights of cold sarcasm. "And his heir."

Garst was both impressed and puzzled. The von Wilmenhorst family owned Sector Four, one of the richest areas of human-occupied space. One day, Helena von Wilmenhorst would control the destinies of over a hundred planets, subject only to the orders of the Throne. "But how did she get here and what does she want?" he mused aloud.

"As to the first," Lady A drawled, "I imagine it must be some flaw in this vaunted organization you've been telling me about. She is hardly the sort of character we

12

should be catering to, and I suspect someone along the way was bribed to let her come. As to the second . . ." She paused to consider something, and finally decided to trust Garst enough to say it.

"As to the second, you will have to know one additional fact about her father: Zander von Wilmenhorst is the Head of the Service of the Empire."

Garst stared at her in disbelief. The Service of the Empire, or SOTE, was virtually the right arm of the Emperor himself. It was the most elite intelligence gathering network ever assembled by mankind, dedicated to enforcing Imperial policies and staffed only by the most loyal, most talented agents in the Galaxy.

Lady A saw his confusion and, for the first time since he'd known her, she smiled. It was a smile that offered no warmth or comfort. "That fact is not generally known," she added, "and it would not be wise to spread it beyond these walls."

"SOTE." Garst's mind raced as he considered the possibilities. "That means she's here to investigate us."

"The lightning swiftness of your mind never fails to astonish me."

He ignored Lady A's irony as he hurriedly punched out an order on his desk computer. Within seconds, a printout of the Hazel Whiting file issued from the tiny slot at the side of his desk. He gave it a careful perusal while his companion eyed him with patient curiosity.

"According to our records, 'Hazel Whiting' first applied to us on the planet Kiesel in Sector Five. She approached one of our agents, claiming to be a jewel thief and swindler. Her reason for asking to come to Sanctuary was that her partner was killed during their last job, and that there were enough clues pointing to her involvement in some seventy capers that she was sure SOTE would be on her trail as well as the regular police. She claims to have attended some of Sector Five's

13

better schools, and she's obviously several levels above the usual rank of people we get here." Garst scrutinized the record a little more carefully. "I don't see much corroboration of her story here—my man seems to have taken a great deal of it on faith. Or perhaps he took a great deal of it on credit. In any event, I shall have him replaced immediately."

Garst stood up and began to pace around slowly behind his desk. He was quite conscious now of Lady A's eyes focused on him. She was observing him like a specimen under a microscope, and he had the feeling that his future employment would hinge largely on how he chose to cope with this latest development.

"Putting aside for the moment the question of how she got here," he said carefully, "we still face the problem of what to do with her now that she's here."

"Indeed." Lady A's brusque comment implied that she wanted to see how he would react to the threat. Garst suddenly found himself perspiring heavily, even though his office was comfortably cool.

He decided to enumerate the possibilities. "We could kill her, we could take her in and give her a shot of nitrobarb to see what she knows, or we could let her wander around, keeping her under close observation to see what she does and whom she contacts.

"I'm opposed to the first alternative for aesthetic reasons. Killing is a last resort, because all the information she has would be lost. It's a move of panic and desperation; so far, the threat she poses is not that serious. Killing her is the safest thing we could do, but not necessarily the smartest.

"The second alternative is very attractive. There's no way anyone can lie under nitrobarb; she would tell us everything we needed to know about how she discovered us, how she managed to get here, what her plans

14

are and how SOTE plans to deal with us. Even if she died under questioning, we would still benefit."

"Yet I seem to detect a note of hesitation in your voice," Lady A observed. "If giving her nitrobarb has all those advantages, why not do it and get it over with?"

"Several reasons. Suppose she's here to contact someone else, someone whom she doesn't know, but who will get in touch with her using a code phrase of some sort. It wouldn't do us any good to pick her up in that case, since it would only scare off her contact. By letting her play on our leash, we may make a bigger haul of infiltrators. Then too, by keeping her alive, we may be able to use her as a bargaining point later, should any trouble arise. The longer we're able to string her out, the more we may learn."

"This method is the least secure of your three alternatives," Lady A pointed out.

"Yes, but potentially the most rewarding. And the threat she poses is still minimal. There's no way she can broadcast a message off this planet using our equipment without our knowledge, and I'll have her belongings screened thoroughly—and discreetly—to make sure she has no transmitters on her. The only way to get offplanet is aboard our ships, and I'll quadruple the guard on the spaceport to make sure she doesn't sneak by us that way."

"What's to stop any of her offworld friends from landing one of their own ships secretly and meeting her?"

Garst smiled. "This planet is well off the main trade lanes, and as you know is listed in the Empire's files as having been explored and passed over for settlement. The only ships that should be coming anywhere near here are our own, and we know the schedule. Anything else that comes within the boundaries of this solar system is blasted instantly out of the skies. We control all access in and out—of that much, I'm sure."

Lady A was silent for a moment. Garst scanned her impassive face, trying to read approval or disapproval in her eyes. Had he passed the test and retained her confidence, or had he made some error in logic that would brand him as incompetent?

At last the woman spoke. "Very well, Garst, I agree with your reasoning. Putting Helena von Wilmenhorst under nitrobarb would gain us very little, in the long run. We already have our own access to most of the information she could tell us about SOTE's operations in general; and in regard to the specific mission she's on now, you can do just as well by keeping her under tight surveillance. But you'd better make sure that surveillance *is* tight—no holes, no leaks, no way for her to escape." The *or else* implied in her tone of voice was entirely too obvious.

"No need to worry about that. Every room in her apartment will be thoroughly searched and monitored around the clock by my best security people. Beepers will be placed in all her clothing. Wherever she goes, there will be two people on her tail. We'll keep lists of everyone she contacts, under what circumstances the contacts were made, and we'll have tails put on all those contacts who look even the faintest bit suspicious. I'll personally review the progress of the investigation at least once a day, to make sure there are no slip-ups. Gospozha von Wilmenhorst will be given more surveillance than the entire Imperial family. Nothing will slip by us, I'll stake my life on that."

"Yes," said Lady A, "you very well may."

After his visitor had gone and he had ordered the implementation of his surveillance tactics, Garst sat alone in his office, deep in thought. *What have I gotten myself into?* he wondered. *Exactly whom have I allied myself with?*

He reached across his desk and fiddled with the controls of his recorder. As a matter of routine he taped every meeting held in this office, so that they could be played back to refresh his memory. Now, as he sat behind the desk with the lights dimmed, he watched the ghostly images come to life and repeat the performance of earlier that afternoon.

Certain phrases haunted him. "That particular plum has been within my reach before," referring to the Throne. And again, "we already have our own access to most of the information she could tell us about SOTE's operations in general."

After his faked death and hasty departure from the gambling moon Vesa, Garst had desperately utilized all the contacts he knew in the Galaxy's underworld until, through the friend of a friend of a friend, he had gotten in touch with this Lady A and asked for a job. He had expected to be integrated into a criminal organization and allowed to use his talents there; but Lady A's conversation left him little doubt that he was actually connected to an Empire-wide conspiracy of infinitely vaster proportions. The thought of what this could mean filled him with both terror and eager anticipation.

Garst was a particularly ambitious man. Until recently, his ambitions had been thwarted by being confined to a single small satellite; but now, the prospect of true power was blossoming before him. He found its aroma intoxicating.

He got up and walked around to the front of his desk, fingering gently the small medallion he had been given when he joined the organization. It was a membership badge, he had been told then, a form of identification. In form, it was quite simple: a tiny integrated

17

circuit chip on a thin golden chain, almost invisible unless someone looked closely. But it made him part of something that obviously spanned the Galaxy and had as its goal supreme control of the human race.

Garst knew he would never be content to be a cog in someone else's wheel. He would have to find the stepladder to the top of this power structure and climb it rapidly. He might not wind up as the big boss of the machine, but he knew he was capable of greater things than this.

There would be obstacles, of course. Although he'd been put in charge of this entire planet, not a single member of his staff was personally loyal to him. They'd all been picked by Lady A; even Jinda Rawling, his security chief and top aide, would probably throw her lot in with Lady A if her devotion should ever be put to the test. That meant Garst would have to work alone. No one else could be completely trusted if he were to achieve his aims. But still, he knew he could do it.

Helena von Wilmenhorst could prove the key to his upward mobility. Although he had been careful to mention nothing about it to Lady A, that was another of his motives for keeping that young lady alive and under close scrutiny. He wasn't sure how yet, but the young duchess might prove useful to him in his upward climb.

The thought was exhilarating.

CHAPTER 2

Mission on Mellisande

The planet Mellisande had five moons that danced an elaborate waltz through its nighttime skies. The largest was more than half the size of Earth's own moon, and two of the others were almost as big, which meant that the nights on Mellisande were seldom dark. A silvery glow pervaded the atmosphere, lending a fairy tale aura to even the most mundane of settings. When all the moons were up at once, the night could be nearly half as bright as the day.

At present, though, only one large and one small moon were above the horizon, for which the two shadow-shapes currently creeping through the bushes were extremely grateful. Their job would be difficult enough without having to run the risk of being spotted in excessively bright moonlight.

The scene below them was a tranquil one: a large manor house set out in the country more than two kilometers from its neighbors, with open land surrounding it on three sides. Its back was built against a cliff face that rose fifty meters into the air. The cliff front was so smooth that it was judged unclimbable, leaving the occupants of the house secure in the knowledge that they could not be attacked from that direction.

The two shadows hoped the inhabitants felt *very* secure; it would help them immensely.

They lay prone side by side for several minutes on

top of the cliff, studying the layout below them. Ten cars were parked in front of the manor house. As they watched, an eleventh car made its appearance, driving up the narrow dirt road from the main highway and pulling to a stop beside the others. Two people got out and walked to the front door of the house. After a few moments of waiting on the doorstep, they were permitted to enter.

"That should be all of them," said one of the shadows in a deep, masculine voice.

The other shadow, a female, nodded in response. "*Alors*, let's stop lolling about and get to work."

The man stood up and lifted a device that looked very much like a harpoon gun. As he hefted it and focused its sights, his companion took a length of carlon rope from her utility belt and tied it onto a stake that had been driven securely into the ground near the edge of the cliff. "Ready," she said.

The man took aim with his weapon and fired. The harpoon shot out of the gun and flew downward toward the roof of the house. Its plastic-bulbed tip shattered in the cranny between the chimney and the sloping roof, releasing a gummy white liquid that solidified immediately upon contact with the air. The instaweld formed a permanent bond between the rooftop and the spear; only the use of a special solvent would remove the harpoon from its new resting place.

The only sound so far had been the small but unavoidable pop of the harpoon's tip as it came in contact with the building. The two people at the top of the cliff waited breathlessly to see whether there was any reaction from inside the house. When none came after three minutes, they let out silent sighs of relief; the rest of their mission could be accomplished much more quietly.

With rapid efficiency, the man pulled the slack out of the line attached to the harpoon. Then, with the merest of nods to his companion, he grabbed hold of the rope and began lowering himself in a quick hand-over-hand motion to the roof of the house so far below them.

The woman stood patiently at the top, watching her comrade make his descent and staying ever alert for trouble. While the man was traveling down the rope, he would be an exposed target, and she would have to guard him. As soon as he reached his destination, he signaled up to her and she began her own descent, while he returned the favor and kept watch for her.

The total transfer time to the rooftop was less than five minutes. The instant they were both together, they wasted no time setting their attack plans into motion. They had preselected one window as their primary point of entrance; moving swiftly and silently to the east side of the steeply slanting roof, the man lay prone holding another, shorter length of carlon rope. The woman took hold of the free end and began lowering herself over the edge to determine whether the window was unlocked or guarded by alarms.

All this work with ropes and climbing was hardly new to these two people; indeed, their familiarity with the equipment was almost inbred. The woman was Yvette d'Alembert, and the man was her brother Jules, and until slightly over a year ago they had been the premier aerialists in the entire Empire. As the star performers of the Circus of the Galaxy, they had been dangling from ropes and swinging on trapezes since babyhood.

But the job they were engaged in this night had nothing to do with trivial entertainment. Their real employment was as the top secret agents in the Service of the Empire. They and their entire circus family were among the ablest and most loyal servants the Crown could wish for; they had proven their worth repeatedly, and asked

21

for little more than the honor of serving again in the future.

As Yvette dangled alongside the window they had chosen, she examined it carefully. It was locked by a simple turnbolt from the inside, and there were no alarms on it that her sophisticated pocket sensors could detect. Pulling herself tightly against the wall, she managed to slide the bolt and pry the window open. From that point, it was a simple matter to grab onto the sill and pull herself into the room. The inside of this chamber was dark and still. It appeared to be a guest bedroom, but was not in use at the moment. As soon as her preliminary check indicated that it was safe, she gave a single sharp tug on the rope to let her brother know it was all right to follow.

Up on the roof, Jules secured the rope by the simple expedient of breaking another small vial of instaweld at the spot where the line dangled over the eaves. As soon as he ascertained that the material had done its job, he scrambled down the rope and, within a minute, was standing beside his sister. Both agents had their stunguns out and ready for action.

Moving with superlative stealth, they padded over to the doorway, opened it a crack and gazed out into the hallway beyond. The hall was unfortunately well lit, but at least was deserted. At the far end of the corridor they could see the staircase that they would have to use to go downstairs where their quarries awaited. Between their present location and the stairs were three closed and two open doors.

The first two rooms they came to were empty. In the third, they encountered a couple of servants engaged in amorous pursuits; Yvette felt like a terrible spoilsport as she gave them number four stuns that would knock them out for two solid hours, but she knew her action was necessary. They could not afford to leave anyone behind them to sound the alarm; they could fight more effectively on only one front. Whispering an apology that the unconscious couple would never hear, she closed the door on them once more to restore their privacy.

In the fourth room a man sat at a desk with his back to the door, engaged in writing. The two shadows crossing the doorway startled him and he turned quickly to see who his visitors were—but that was the last action he took for several hours. Jules's lightning reflexes stunned the man down where he was sitting without allowing him the chance to cry out in alarm.

The fifth room was again empty, and they came at last to the stairway. The two d'Alemberts exchanged brief, encouraging glances. So far, all had gone smoothly; but from this point onward, they could expect trouble at any second. As nearly as they could figure it, there were at least two dozen people still occupying the lower floors of the house. The odds against the agents' catching *all* of them off guard were pretty high. They would have a fight on their hands before they were done this evening—but they had expected that and were prepared for it. Their enemies were not.

The time for stealth had passed; speed would now be their best weapon. At the tiniest nod from Jules, both of them took off down the stairs side-by-side at top speed, streaks of fury moving at a rate that would have seemed impossible for normal human beings to attain.

But then, the d'Alemberts were not exactly normal human beings. For more than ten generations their family had resided on the planet DesPlaines, a world of heavy metals and forbidding mountains with a surface gravity three times higher than that of Earth. Weaklings were weeded out in the first two generations by the planet's harsh conditions. The current inhabitants of DesPlaines were all superstrong and superfast. They had to be—merely standing up and walking around in such a gravitational field would tax the energies of normal people, not to mention the fact that, on a world where objects would fall at three times the terrestrial rate of acceleration, a survivor had to have lightning reflexes. There was hardly any such thing as a "minor" accident on DesPlaines. Those who survived were definitely the fittest.

But their genetic background was shared by more than seven million other inhabitants of their home world. What made Jules and Yvette stand out even further was the family heritage of the d'Alemberts, the long line of circus performers that traced all the way back to the founding of the Circus of the Galaxy. Physical training and agility had been the keynote of their education from the moment of their birth; now, at the very peak of their careers, Jules and Yvette were the most perfect physical specimens humanity could hope to produce.

Little wonder, then, that the two SOTE agents came flying down the stairs at speeds calculated to dazzle the unsuspecting people they were hunting. The middle floor of the house was populated by the servants, who were banished to this level to be out of the way of the bigwigs conferring on the ground floor. They were small fry being caught in the d'Alemberts' net, of no strategic value, but they had to be stunned anyway; they would otherwise fight to protect the safety of the house, and a fight was the last thing the DesPlainian siblings wanted.

As Jules raced into the final room on this floor, he spotted a servant standing beside a basin. He fired his stunner on pure reflex, realizing at the instant he shot that the woman was drinking a glass of water. The glass fell from the woman's hand and, quick as Jules's reflexes were, he still could not catch it before it hit the floor. The glass shattered with a sound that seemed to fill the entire universe with its noise.

There was no help for it—the alarm was out now. The people downstairs would have heard the sound and would be on edge until some explanation was forthcoming. Even though they would not be expecting a full-scale assault, they would be on the defensive and not nearly such easy pickings as the servants had been.

As Yvette and Jules rushed back to the stairway to continue their descent into the house, neither said a word. They didn't have to; the two had worked together as a team for so many years, with their lives literally depending on their split-second precision, that their minds functioned as a single unit. They both knew what had to be done, and each knew precisely how the other would react to any conceivable circumstance.

As they raced down the stairs in tandem, twin blurs against the powder blue wallpaper, a head peered out from a doorway, obviously curious about the crashing noise from upstairs. The man's eyes widened at the sight of the two forms dashing down the steps, and he let out a yelp of astonishment. Yvette fired her stunner, but the man was just able to duck back out of sight, and begin sounding the alarm in earnest. The battle royal had begun.

The stairs ended at the front of a hallway, with a large living room to the left and a slightly smaller salon to the right. Jules turned without hesitation toward the living room, leaving the other side of the house to the capable hands of his sister.

As he entered the room, Jules looked an imposing foe indeed. His body was short, as was typical of Des-Plainians—only 173 centimeters tall—but he was solidly muscled and not a man to be regarded casually. He was dressed in a gray jumpsuit (he and Yvette having decided that gray would offer better camouflage under the moons of Mellisande than dead black) and the tight cut of the clinging fabric emphasized all the bulging muscles of his hundred kilogram body. He turned his head back and forth quickly, further ruffling his short brown hair, as his steel gray eyes scanned the room to size up the situation.

There were seven people in the living room, five men and two women. All of them were familiar to him from pictures he had studied. They were the major leaders of this world's criminal underground; a list of the offenses committed by just these seven people would have been taller than Jules, and each of them represented an organization that multiplied their powers manyfold.

The closest person to the doorway was a man seated in a great chair. As Jules's fleeting form burst into the room, this man started to rise from his seat, one hand reaching into his coat pocket for a weapon. It was a move he never completed. Jules grabbed the man's hand before it could reach the holster; using his own forward momentum and the man's rising movement, he yanked the hapless gangster to his feet. That pull helped slow Jules down and, expert athlete that he was, he used that to his advantage. With his unwilling accomplice as an axis, Jules whirled around once, then planted his feet and swung the man around instead. The man was lifted off his feet and flew heavily through the air, colliding with another man and woman across the room and knocking them all to the ground, unconscious. Jules was not specifically a weightlifter—his cousin Rick could have performed the same feat a lot more effortlessly—but his powerful DesPlainian body could still put a lot of force behind his movements, and the result was most gratifying.

By this time, though, the other four people in the room had been alerted enough to draw their own weapons—blasters, Jules noted quickly. These people did

26

not play around with halfway measures. They would rather scorch some of the wallpaper than let him get away with the effrontery of this invasion.

Jules's reflexes were faster, though. Stun-gun in hand, he downed two of the men across the room before having to duck to avoid the blaster beam that sizzled the air above his head. He turned his dodging motion into a low flat dive and a roll that brought him into collision with the knees of the last remaining male. The fellow was knocked off his feet and tumbled over Jules's body, thereby receiving a blaster bolt intended for Jules. There was only one foe left, a middle-aged woman with a steely glint in her eyes and a burning blaster in her hand.

Under the proper circumstances, Jules could be as chivalrous as the most gallant courtier. But niceties such as not shooting a woman did not apply when that woman was trying to kill him. Raising his stunner once more, he squeezed off a shot that dropped the woman in her tracks before she had a chance to correct her aim. He looked around quickly, making sure there were no other foes in the vicinity, then got to his feet and raced out to see if his sister needed any help.

As she ran into the salon, Yvette d'Alembert looked hardly less formidable than her brother. Though ten centimeters shorter and thirty kilos lighter, her body was still of the sturdy DesPlainian stock. The gray jumpsuit that she, too, wore emphasized all the best aspects of her feminine form. She was a sight that would be pleasing to the eyes of any man—except one who had to come up against her in combat.

She found five antagonists waiting for her as she entered the room, all men. Two of them she was able to dispose of immediately with her own stun-gun before she had to start dodging the blaster beams that the other three were employing liberally.

27

She dived behind one large, overstuffed chair to avoid a beam that would otherwise have hit her at chest level. Taking advantage of her cover, she shot down another of her foes, and the remaining pair bolted. One of them tried to make it out the door, but Yvette was not going to allow that. Lifting the massive chair off the ground, she threw it with all her strength at the fleeing criminal. The man's blaster burned a hole through the upholstery, but couldn't slow the heavy object in its flight path. The impact of its weight knocked him hard against the wall, where he crumpled to the floor, unconscious.

Throwing the chair left Yvette devoid of cover against the beams of the final gangster. She twisted away frantically as one bolt went by. It caught the edge of her gun, heating the stunner so much that Yvette could not hold onto it. She dropped the gun and fell behind a low coffee table, on top of which were several items of bric-a-brac.

The last man, thinking his opponent disarmed and helpless, stood up and aimed his blaster carefully; he would take no chances on missing his shot this time. But he reckoned without knowledge of Yvette's resourcefulness and skill. Grabbing a small emerald statuette from the tabletop, the SOTE operative hurled it with all her DesPlainian strength and aerialist's accuracy straight at the face of her enemy. The object hit him in the jaw with a resounding crack of shattered bone, and the man fell backwards onto the floor, out cold.

Yvette was just picking herself up off the floor as her brother raced into the room. He glanced around the room quickly, viewing the carnage, and asked, "Need any help?"

Yvette shook her head. "All smooth. Routine, actually. We'd better check to make sure this is the entire haul."

The two siblings roamed through the rest of the house, but could find no further opponents to face. They went upstairs and devoted the next half hour to tying up the servants securely, in case they should come out of stun while the interrogation was still going on downstairs. Then they returned to the living room and salon and tied up all those captives. After that, there was still almost an hour's wait until the effects of their stunners wore off and the interrogation could begin.

During their last assignment, traces of a widespread conspiracy against the Throne had come to light, with implications that were positively chilling. Duke Fyodor Paskoi, ruler of the planet Kolokov, and his assistant, Dr. Immanuel Rustin, had apparently been creating robots that looked and acted exactly like real people. One of these robots had been used in a plot against Crown Princess Edna, but those plans had been foiled by quick action on the part of the d'Alemberts and their friends.

The problem the Service now faced was to find the rest of these deadly devices and neutralize them. They had no idea how many of them there were, and the duke and the doctor were no longer among the living to be able to divulge that information. No record could be found as to what the robots looked like or where they had been sent—or what their missions could be. The only thing known for certain was that treason would be involved.

The job of tracking down these insidious devices was not an enviable one, which was why the Head had assigned Jules and Yvette, his two best agents, to conduct the investigation. They had an insatiable appetite for work—and the harder the assignment, the better they liked it.

Since Dr. Rustin was the genius behind the actual construction of the robots, the d'Alemberts had concentrated their initial attentions on his actions for the past several years. They discovered that he had made a number of trips here to the planet Mellisande for no apparent purpose. After several more weeks of checking, they discovered that he had frequently been seen in the company of several of the top hoodlums on this world, and that there was to be a big get-together of underworld figures—the perfect opportunity for them to net all their suspects at the same time. It was this path that had led the two superagents to this particular house on this particular night.

With their suspects bound securely, the two Des-Plainians examined them carefully. It was Yvette who first noticed the tiny necklaces that two of them were wearing—integrated circuit chips on golden chains. "Look at these," she called to her brother. "I seem to recall from their description that both Duke Fyodor and Dr. Rustin wore necklaces like these."

Jules came over and gave them his close scrutiny. "*Absolutement,*" he said. "We seem to have found a correlation. Possibly it's some sort of identity code, or has some fraternal significance. Whatever it means, though, it's obvious that we'll have to concentrate most of our efforts on these two. I prescribe nitrobarb for them and detrazine for the rest."

Yvette nodded her concurrence and, from a kit in her belt, she began readying the indicated injections. Both drugs were variations of truth serum; detrazine was by far the more common, although it was possible for a subject with a hypnotic block or an extremely strong willpower to be able to withstand its effects. That was not the case with nitrobarb, the most powerful truth drug known to man. No one could resist telling the complete truth under its influence—but the drawback

30

was that the drug had a fifty percent mortality rate, and was very tricky to use. These disagreeable side effects had led to nitrobarb's being proscribed. Mere possession of it was a capital offense—but that, of course, did not stop people on either side of the law from using it.

It took about twenty minutes for the nitrobarb to take effect. While they waited, Jules and Yvette questioned the mob leaders who were given the faster-acting detrazine. Everything that was said went directly into the d'Alemberts' miniaturized recorders for possible future use by SOTE or other law enforcement agencies. Many subjects were covered, and the agents dug up enough dirt on these underlings to construct several large dams—but there was little information in the area of their particular interest. Some of these people had been introduced to Dr. Rustin and talked to him on social occasions, but either they knew nothing about the conspiracy to which he belonged or else they had blocks in their minds that the detrazine could not penetrate.

By this time, though, the agents' prime targets were all warmed up and ready for them. Slowly, patiently, Yvette, who was the more experienced of the pair at interrogation, picked out the story of the conspiracy— or at least as much as these people knew. It was tantalizing and frustrating at the same time.

Both these men knew about the robot-building program. They personally knew of only four robots that had been constructed, one of which being the one the d'Alemberts had already destroyed. Of the other three, two were female and the other was male. The male and one of the females were built to look like natives of some heavy gravity planet like DesPlaines but—in reply to a sharp question from Yvette—they had not been made to duplicate either of the d'Alemberts. Jules and his sister breathed a quiet sigh at that; the thought had occurred to each of them that perhaps their identities had been discovered and they were scheduled to be surreptitiously replaced. It was a great relief to learn that their covers were still secure.

Neither of the men under the nitrobarb knew what had become of the robots after they were made, leaving the two operatives as much in the dark as they had been before.

On the matter of the conspiracy in general, the men were equally vague. They took their orders not from Rustin, who was on about the same organizational level as themselves, but from a woman they knew only as "Lady A." They had only met her once, and described her as being exquisitely beautiful and as cold as the backside of an asteroid. Orders would come from her occasionally, telling them to do certain things that seemed to make little sense; but they knew they were to carry out their orders to the letter, doing no more and no less. For this they were paid quite well indeed.

Yes, they said, the golden necklaces with the integrated circuit chips were identification symbols of the conspirators. No, they were not sure whether Lady A was in charge of the entire conspiracy or not; they did recall Dr. Rustin mentioning someone else from whom he took orders, and whom he referred to as "he." The d'Alemberts could get no further information on that point, and could not conclude whether the doctor was referring to his lord—Duke Fyodor—or to some other figure in the treasonous hierarchy.

As information went, it was pitifully slight. But it was more than they had arrived with, and so they could count this raid as a success. "It'll take a lot more successes like this before we start getting anywhere, though," Yvette commented sarcastically.

They left the house the same way they had entered, climbing up the rope to the top of the cliff where their groundcar was parked. This vehicle looked vaguely like a flashy sports model Frascati, but was in reality a Mark Forty-One Service Special capable of converting into a private flying craft. The d'Alemberts had utilized it as such to approach this out-of-the-way location, and they did so again in leaving. As they flew along, Jules radioed in to the local SOTE offices, using only his code name, Wombat, and described the situation at the house as they had left it. The thought of the interrogation tapes instantly excited the personnel at the agency, who had been trying to get solid information on these people for quite some time. The tapes would give the local authorities enough clues to definitely nail convictions on each of these gang leaders—and Mellisande would be a cleaner place to live for a while.

The d'Alemberts left the tapes at a safe drop point and continued along the ground to the spaceport where their private two-person ship, *La Comète Cuivré,* was waiting. Its burnished hull was a comforting sight for the pair of tired agents. Jules drove the car up the ramp and snugged it into its special berth in the lower portion of the vessel. The two climbed out of the car, all set to grab a quick shower and catch up on some much-needed sleep.

But they found that sleep was not programmed for them for quite some time yet. On their message recorder, a red light was blinking furiously. Punching the required button, Yvette discovered that the message was from the Head himself, with a Class Five priority. The siblings exchanged worried glances. Class Five was urgent. The message went on to say that they were to beam a scrambled call back to Earth, using the Head's own private number—and that they were to do so immediately upon their return.

CHAPTER 3

The Missing Girl Friday

Their fatigue was pushed to the backs of their minds; the Head's wishes came before their own personal needs. The two agents began the elaborate process of placing an interstellar scramble call back to the Head on Earth, a full hundred and ten parsecs away.

The subether drive, invented by Oliver Fenton Arnold in 2011, had opened the way for the great human exodus from Earth that occurred in the twenty-first century. In the fifty years following Arnold's invention, it was estimated that more than a billion people left Man's home planet for more than five hundred different worlds where they would be free to pursue their individual destinies and philosophies.

But if Arnold's brilliant device had earned him the title "concierge to the Galaxy," it was Anna Sieppi's invention of the subetheric communicator, or subcom, in 2027 that truly made her the "voice of Empire." It was a simple fact that no political grouping spread over most of the Galaxy could hold together without instantaneous communication. The subcom provided that. Though even now, more than four hundred years after its invention, no way had been discovered to bring the process cheaply to the common public, it was nevertheless a godsend to government, industry and the news services. Subetheric communication welded the human-occupied Galaxy into one cohesive unit.

34

The d'Alemberts' ship, though small, nevertheless had its own complete subcom unit. In addition, a small device built into the set would allow messages to be scrambled and deciphered according to the Service's secret codes—which were changed on an average of every two months. The scrambler insured the maximum amount of secrecy possible during communication between the agents in the field and their home base.

After ten minutes of intricate dialing, the triscreen brightened and a three dimensional image of their boss's head and shoulders appeared inside the tiny box. Zander von Wilmenhorst was almost totally bald, and his face was lined with creases that made him look older than his forty-eight years. But the look in his eyes made any viewer instantly aware that this was a man of keen intelligence and insight. As Head of the Service of the Empire, he was the prime security advisor to the Emperor and the master tactician who kept peace among the stars.

He smiled as the images of Jules and Yvette appeared on his own screen. The expression was a warm one, but weary. "Thank you for answering my message so promptly," he said.

"A Class Five priority calls for promptness," Jules replied.

"Yes, but I expected you'd be so busy with your own case that it might take time for you to get around to answering."

"Actually," Yvette said, "we had just wrapped up one stage of our investigation. It'll take us a while to analyze it and formulate our next move. We were going to report to you anyway."

"Then please do so. My business can wait at least until I hear what you've gotten."

With great precision, careful not to omit even the slightest facts, Jules and Yvette filled their boss in on the results of their raid earlier that day. The Head listened silently, but from his expression he was obviously not pleased with the implications of what he was hearing.

"This conspiracy seems to be growing bigger with each new report," he said when his two top operatives were done. "The answers you got point to whole new dimensions. And the fact that those men knew of only four robots doesn't mean there aren't more. It gives us a starting point, but that's about all. It's my job to be paranoid; I *have* to assume that the actual number is much higher until it's proven otherwise.

"Put your findings in writing and beam the report to my office as soon as you can. I'll have our computers correlate it and see if we can develop any new leads for you. But for now, I've got something else for you to work on—something a lot more personal."

He paused and gazed at them. The look in his eyes was one they'd never seen before. Slowly he said, "Helena's disappeared."

The news shocked them both. The d'Alemberts were extremely fond of their boss's daughter. "What? How . . . ?"

"You remember when last you were in my office, I told you I had sent her on vacation for a while. She was overworking herself, and she's still too young for that sort of thing. I insisted that she get away for a month or two, to let herself wind down.

"At first I heard from her nearly every day. She kept calling and telling me how guilty she felt leaving me to run the office here by myself—and, to tell you the truth, she did keep it better organized than I've ever been able to. Then, after about two weeks, she stopped calling. I figured she'd finally resigned herself to enjoying her vacation, so I put it to the back of my mind. But

36

after two months without any further word, my fatherly concern got the better of me.

"I did some preliminary checking on my own. My last contact with her had been on the planet Evanoe. As it happens, Marask Kantana had been on that planet at the same time, so I called her to find out if she knew anything. You remember her, don't you?"

Indeed they did. When they first met her, Marask Kantana had been the Service's planetary chief of Chandakha; but she had proven so capable in that position that she was afterwards promoted to a job as special executive troubleshooter for the Head himself. It was her particular assignment to travel around and attempt to spot problems before they turned into major security headaches.

"Certainly," Jules replied to the Head's question. "How is she?"

"Fine. And she seems to be working out well in her job, too—she's spotted several tiny problems that we were able to nip before they developed into cancers. She had been writing a report about one on Evanoe when Helena arrived there. The two of them had lunch together the day of Helena's last contact with me, and Kantana explained the problem to her. She told me that Helena had seemed very excited about it, and kept pressing her for details—and since Helena was one of my chief aides, she told her everything.

"At about that point, I recalled what you had told me when you were last in my office—that Helena was eager to do some field work, and was anxious to share some of the so-called glamour of the espionage game instead of being just an office worker."

"And you think she took it into her head to work on this case herself." Yvette's tone made her words into more of a statement than a question.

"Exactly. I think she wanted to show her poor old

father that she could do something more than just be a superefficient secretary." He sighed. "Some people never learn to stick with what they do best—or if they do learn, it comes the hard way."

"How much training has she had?" Jules asked.

"She's been through the Academy with good marks in everything, so she's well up on theory. She's had plenty of education in weapons and fighting, so she can take care of herself in most normal situations. She scored 948 on the thousand-point test, so her potential is there. But she has no practical experience. Even when I sent the two of you out on your first major assignment against Banion's forces, you had at least lived all your lives with the rest of your family and knew the ropes pretty well from hearing their stories. Your father in particular is a superb teacher; if he weren't so important to me right where he is, I'd put him in charge of our Academy to see that our agents are taught correctly.

"Helena's never had the practical kind of experience she needs to handle something of this magnitude. She's read a lot of reports about how agents have behaved under stress—but it's one thing to read about it happening to someone else, and quite another to know how to react when you're in the middle of a situation yourself. That's the only thing that has me worried—Helena's still a little too naive to do the job right." He paused and gave his head a wry little shake. "That and the fact that I need her back here. The detail work is getting out of hand, and it takes three other people to handle her position. I have plenty of agents who can work in the field; I need someone here who can keep my office in order."

"I take it, then," Yvette said, "that you want us to find her, spank her and bring her back."

"Find her, yes—several of my lesser agents have already tried and failed, which is why I'm bothering you with my problems. But as for the rest—well, field experience won't necessarily hurt her since, as I told you before, I'm training her to take over my position someday. It'll do her some good to know what goes on in the outside universe; she'll be able to understand her agents' problems better. But I have to make sure she isn't in over her head. After all, she is privy to about ninety-nine percent of everything that goes on in our organization. Her knowledge in the wrong hands could destroy us—so our not knowing exactly where she is represents a potentially serious breach of security. Especially since she knows your identities and the role of the Circus in our arsenal."

The two DesPlainians nodded. Only a handful of people outside the d'Alembert family knew of the Circus's involvement with SOTE. Security was so tight that there was no written record of the connection between the two in any of the Empire's vast data banks. The Circus was the ultimate weapon SOTE had for dealing with plots and treason—and Helena was one of the people who knew about that. If that information fell into anyone else's hands, centuries of hard work and security would be undone.

"What I would like you to do," the Head continued, "is, after you find her, make sure she's capable of handling whatever she's found. If everything's smooth, let her be, it'll do her good. If she needs help, give it to her—you're the best I've got. And if she's in way over her head, get her out of there as quickly as possible. That's essentially it."

But the pair of agents could detect something more in his face. His words were those of a boss concerned with the safety of one of his employees; but, written clearly in his eyes, were the words of a father worried desperately about his daughter. *Make sure she's safe and alive*, he was saying, *and make sure she stays that way*.

"I've arranged to have Marask brief you on the problem," said the Head. "She can give you the details better than I can, since she's closer to it and has been working on it longer. You can call her at SOTE headquarters on Evanoe. I've already told her to expect to hear from you. She'll have a report all ready."

Yvette wanted to reach out and pat her boss's hand, telling him things would be all right. Unfortunately, that was impossible over a separation of a hundred and ten parsecs, so she had to settle for saying, "We'll do our best, sir."

"I know," he smiled back. "And thanks." He cut the connection, and the screen faded slowly to black.

Yvette fixed the two of them a quick snack in the ship's small but efficient galley while Jules fiddled with the controls of the subcom trying to raise Marask Kantana on the planet Evanoe. It was difficult getting in touch with her because the executive assistant had no permanent number at which she could be reached. Adding to the problem was the fact that it was several hours before dawn at SOTE headquarters on that world, and the staff on duty there were not the top flight people.

But what helped cut through most of the red tape was Jules's use of his and Yvette's code names: Wombat and Periwinkle. Those two names were practically legendary throughout the Service; there was not a single SOTE employee who would not drop everything at once to obey the orders he received from either of those two people. Thus, even though Jules kept his visual transmitter turned off, his words prompted instant attention. Altogether, it took twenty minutes to establish a linkup with the still sleepy Kantana.

Yvette brought the food into the control room just as Marask Kantana's features appeared in the screen. She had obviously been roused from sleep to answer this call; her dark-skinned face was devoid of makeup, making her look slightly older than her actual midforties age. Her black hair, which was gray tipped, was tangled and unkempt, and her compassionate brown eyes were still a bit clouded by sleep. But even under these conditions, the beauty of her soul showed through. "Greetings," she said slowly. "The Head told me you'd be calling, but I had no idea it would be this soon."

"We believe in moving quickly," Yvette told her. "It's good to see you again."

"I wish I could say the same thing—but I understand the reason why I can't." At present, she *wasn't* seeing them. Although she had met both of them, the d'Alemberts still preferred not to transmit their images to a possibly unsecured channel, and so were on audio only. The call, of course, was scrambled.

"We're given to understand that Girl Friday is missing," Jules said, cutting through any further preliminaries. "We need to know your end of it—the Head thought it might be enlightening."

Marask nodded. "When I had lunch with her a couple of months ago, I told her about the unusual case I was studying and she pumped me with all sorts of questions. The two of you might find it quite fascinating, because it involves the disappearence of many people."

Yvette and Jules exchanged startled looks. The case they had investigated on Vesa, where they had first met Marask, was a murder and robbery ring that had been responsible for the disappearance of hundreds of thousands of people over two decades. "Could someone have learned Garst's old game and started it all over again?" Jules asked.

Marask shook her head. "No, this is being played by different rules entirely. The Vesan disappearances were done in a random pattern, and the victims were relatively anonymous. Also, the Vesan conspiracy was confined to a single satellite. In this new case, I've found evidence that it covers at least two dozen worlds. The pattern is decidedly not random, and the people disappearing are quite notorious and highly sought after.

"In short, the top criminals in this portion of space have suddenly started vanishing. I'm not talking about petty crooks and thieves, but the important ones— heads of mobs, bank robbers who pull spectacular jobs, dishonest politicians who are being investigated a little too closely—that sort of criminal, as well as some of their lesser cohorts. Any time the police start closing in on them, they disappear without a trace. On only a couple of worlds, this would be puzzling but hardly noteworthy; but as I've said, I've seen the same picture emerging on twenty-seven different planets under identical circumstances. That's part of my job, to correlate individual items and find the pattern. In this case, the pattern stinks like week-old garbage."

"And your conclusion?" Jules asked.

"Simply this: that some person or organization has gone into the business of hiding fugitives on an interstellar scale. The fugitives are not simply being shuffled from one planet to another; the police are efficient enough to have spotted that. The 'vanishees' are being taken somewhere and kept out of our clutches."

"Which means that somewhere," Yvette said, reading between the lines of the report, "there is a colony of thieves, murderers, grafters and general nogoodniks being established. While I'm sure there's a great deal of profit in offering these people sanctuary, I'm wondering whether there might not also be some ulterior motive involved."

42

"That thought had crossed my mind as well," Marask commented.

"Think of it," Yvette said, more as musing aloud than as conversation. "A colony full of some of the most successful criminals in this part of the Galaxy. They would provide fantastic raw material for any conspiracy interested in more than just breaking the law and making a little bit of profit."

"A breeding ground for treason," Jules agreed. "It's a possibility we don't dare overlook. As the Head remarked, we're paid to be a little paranoid."

"And it's not hard to see how this would have appealed to Girl Friday," Yvette continued. She was not about to break Helena's cover by mentioning her name over the subcom. "By posing as some sort of criminal, she would get them to accept her into their sanctuary, wherever it is. Once there, she would try to learn as much as she could, then break out and bring the knowledge back to headquarters."

"If she *can* break out," Jules said. "Whoever has set this system up would make security his number one concern. Getting in could be managed with the right connections, but getting out again would be an entirely different matter. She could find herself trapped in there with no way of escape."

Kantana nodded. "That's how I read her situation. I didn't know she had vanished until the Head called me a couple of days ago, but given all that I know and the persistence with which she asked her questions, I should think it's fairly obvious what's happened."

The conversation continued on for another hour, with the d'Alemberts pressing the executive assistant for more details about the disappearances. When they were finally satisfied that they knew all that was officially known, they thanked Marask for her help and told her not to worry further—they would take the matter from here.

"Telling her not to worry really won't do any good," Yvette said as the other woman's features faded off the triscreen. "A good agent worries about everything until the case is finally disposed of—and Marask is one hell of a good agent."

"I know," Jules agreed. "And there's a lot to worry about. From the way she described these disappearances, the gang behind them is a group of top-notch professionals. They'll take no risks at all. If Helena gives them even one good reason to suspect her, they could kill her out of hand. They've got some of the best criminal talent in the Galaxy working with them, and they won't hesitate to protect their interests. Particularly if, as we suspect, they've got some further plans in mind for the future."

"So we've got to form some plans of our own for infiltrating them and finding Helena. The obvious ploy is to pretend to be outside the law ourselves so that the people we want will be interested in us as well."

"Not pretend," Jules corrected. "We're going to have to actually *be* criminals, with a solid record of accomplishment behind us. I don't want to have any holes in our story at all if we're going to walk into this particular lion's den in broad daylight."

"That sounds vaguely like a mixed metaphor, but I catch your meaning. We're going to be scrutinized pretty closely, and if we have to perform a rescue mission our credentials must be above reproach."

Although both were tired from their raid earlier that evening, they knew that neither would be able to sleep until they had at least outlined their plans for saving Helena. For the next three hours they batted ideas back and forth, discarding the bad ones and refining the good until at last their plan of attack took on a definite shape in their minds.

Only then could they allow themselves a few hours of deep sleep before embarking for their new destination more than two hundred parsecs away in an entirely different sector of the Galaxy.

CHAPTER 4

Cat-Burglars of Cordoba

The planet Cordoba was a relatively prosperous one. With a population of better than nine hundred million scattered over three large continents, there was no threat of overcrowding and its attendant evils. Large areas of fertile land were given over to agriculture, but that still left much room for virgin wilderness. Industry was high enough to maintain self-sufficiency without becoming a burden on the environment. No city had more than two million inhabitants, and only thirty-four on the entire world had more than a million.

The people of Cordoba had their share of problems, but on the whole they were satisfied with their lot. In the official files of the Service of the Empire, Cordoba was listed as a very stable planet, low on the list of potential trouble spots.

Avila, the capital city of the planet, was ruled by a baroness. Though her rank was technically the lowest level of nobility, being ruler of the capital city gave her influence that extended beyond her title, and a tax base many earls, who controlled larger areas, would envy. The Baroness of Avila was considered to be one of the wealthiest people on Cordoba.

Being a woman of taste and culture, the Baroness preferred to invest her money in works of art and jewelry rather than commercial enterprises. She had a unique collection of emerald and gold jewelry, including a ten-piece set that had been crafted particularly to her order and whose total weight was more than three thousand carats. Also, in one particular gallery, she had hung the complete miniatures of the renowned artist Mastrovnaya—seventeen pieces in all, at an insured value of over ninety thousand rubles. Her manor house, Casa Avila, was one of the showplaces of the planet.

On this particular evening, eight days after the Head had talked with the d'Alemberts, the Baroness was away from home attending a charity function. She was not especially worried about the safety of her property, since Casa Avila was guarded by numerous electronic devices and an army of security guards. The jewels and art were safe from even reasonably skilled thieves—but few defenses short of an armored fortress would keep out a certain pair of well-trained DesPlainians.

The smooth metal wall that surrounded the estate was four meters high and electrically charged with enough voltage to stun the strongest constitution. The two SOTE agents, clad in black leather jumpsuits and black satin hoods, came racing toward the wall from the wooded area that adjoined the Baroness's estate. Just before reaching the barrier, they bent their legs under them and leaped in unison. Their two bodies arcing through the air easily cleared the top of the wall. Like the trained aerialists they were, they landed on their feet with their legs tucked under them, expended the rest of the momentum from their leap in a forward somersault, sprang to their feet in one continuous motion and kept on running. Their pace would have looked like a leisurely gait, yet they were covering the distance at nearly fifteen meters a second.

They had picked a spot far from the house to go over the wall, since the security guards were likely to be less numerous there. They moved silently as well as quickly through the darkness, and reached the side of the main building in less than a minute. So far, they had progressed like two phantoms in the night, and had not been spotted.

They scouted the side of the house cautiously, keeping an eye out both for guards and for a good point of entrance. They found a second-story window with an overhanging sill that would suit their purposes admirably. As Jules planted himself firmly under the window, Yvette backed off from him a dozen meters, then ran toward him at top speed. As she leaped, he went into a crouch; catching her in his cupped hands, he straightened up again, lending his full strength to the effort of pushing her upward. His toughened muscles, trained to a gravity three times as strong as this one, vaulted her easily into the air, and she grabbed the window ledge with a strong, sure grip. After peeking inside to make sure the room was empty, she took one gripper from her belt and attached it alongside the window with one hand while continuing to hold onto the sill with her other. The gripper was a simple metal rod held tightly to the wall by two suction cups. When that was done, she attached her second gripper to the other side of the window, then laced a sturdy strap between them. Pulling herself up between them, she now had a backstrap to lean against, like a window washer, while she worked on the delicate task of bypassing the alarm circuits and opening the window.

Jules waited for her in the shadows at the base of the house, his sharp eyes sweeping the scene constantly for signs that their presence had been detected. In Cordoba's moonless night it was almost impossible to see anything. He heard a swishing of air coming at him rapidly from his left and, on instinct, fired his stunner at the charging object. There was a slight gasp and whatever it was collapsed on the ground. Jules decided to risk moving away from the wall for a second to find out what it was.

By putting his hands down on the dark lump in front of him, he could tell that it was the size of a large dog, but the texture of its fur was definitely not canine. Its mouth contained a double set of sharp teeth; Jules shuddered at the thought of how much damage a creature like that could inflict on an unwary victim. That it was some kind of sentry creature he had no doubt at all; but fortunately it seemed to be mute. Its value lay in attacking an intruder and disabling or killing him before he was aware of it, rather than in sending up an alarm. Jules's stun-gun had been set on three, which would be a twenty-minute stun for a human being. Because this creature was smaller than a man, it would probably be out somewhat longer. Jules resolved to keep an even closer eye out for more of those things. The idea of those teeth sinking into his legs was not a pleasant one.

"Are you all right?" Yvette's voice sounded in his ears. They were both wearing miniature receivers and sensitive throat mikes to pick up their subvocalizations and broadcast to each other. "I heard a stunner buzz."

"I hit the local equivalent of a watchdog. They're silent but vicious, and they've got sharp teeth, so be careful."

"All set with the window," Yvette said a few seconds later. She opened it and climbed in, then lowered a rope for her brother. Within another thirty seconds, he was standing beside her inside the house.

Jules and Yvette had an advantage over normal cat burglars in that they had visited this house before. Six years ago, the Circus had played on Cordoba and they, as two of the show's top stars, had been invited to visit and see the Baroness's collection. They had never dreamed then that they would be able to put the experience to such practical use.

49

They went to the door of the room and opened it a tiny crack. The hallway beyond was brightly lighted, and there would be guards patrolling it every few minutes. Both agents had their stunners set on three for a twenty-minute stun. It would be the most humane way of dealing with the opposition; they didn't want to hurt anyone if they could avoid it. Any guard they ran into would have a short nap and be groggy for a little while after that, but there would be no other ill effects. Twenty minutes, meanwhile, would be all they'd need to accomplish their task.

On a signal from Jules, Yvette flung the door wide open and the two DesPlainians dashed out into the hallway. As they had prearranged, Yvette headed directly for the jewels while her brother went after the collection of miniatures.

Yvette ran into a guard as she turned a corner and began to go downstairs. The startled man had no time to react, though, before Yvette's superfast reflexes had caused her to fire her stun-gun. The man crumpled silently into a heap on the floor and Yvette continued on without even slowing down.

The jewel room door was guarded by a pair of men, but neither of those worthies had time to do more than register his astonishment before Yvette's flashing form swept into view and her stunner buzzed twice more. Inside the room, another two guards were overcome just as easily and quickly. It was not that all these people were incompetent at their jobs, but merely that they were caught completely by surprise by someone whose reflexes they could not have matched.

The emerald collection was spread out in three separate "diamont" crystal display cases, and each case had its own individual alarm system. It took Yvette a full ten minutes to circumvent all the alarms, but once that was done the jewels were hers for the taking. Smashing the superhard crystal with her special black-gloved fist, she quickly scooped the priceless gems into a velvet bag. Once that was completed, she raced back out the way she had come. She met no further opposition as she returned to the upstairs room through which she had originally entered.

There was no sign of her brother, but they had agreed not to wait for each other. In three bounding strides she was across the room and standing by the window. Looking down, she thought she detected something moving at the base of the house and, mindful of Jules's warning about the watchdogs, fired a couple of stunner shots down into the darkness. There was a slight sigh, indicating she had hit her target. She tied her bag of loot firmly around her waist and scrambled quickly down the rope to the ground. Once safely on solid footing, she raced off toward the nearest point of the wall. Detection was a secondary consideration now; the speed of her departure was more important. She met no further resistance and made the leap over the wall with the same ease as before. She then sprinted for the d'Alembert groundcar, which had been parked on a small side road more than a kilometer from the Baroness's estate.

Jules was not yet there, but that was to be expected. The paintings he was after were bulkier than her jewels, and dismantling the alarms connected to them would take a little longer. Yvette waited patiently and, seven minutes later, Jules came running toward the vehicle. Yvette started the motor as her brother leaped inside and, within seconds, their "car" was airborne and flying at top speed back to the spaceport.

Jules shot his sister a quick smile. "I think we should congratulate each other on our success," he said.

"If we don't, who will?" Yvette's voice was equally

51

brimming with exhilaration. The thought of a job well done always stimulated them.

Leaning back in his seat, Jules interlocked the fingers of both hands behind his head. "I think, sister dear, that we are about to acquire a reputation around here."

Jules's prophecy turned out to be a magnificent understatement. The story of the daring cat burglars who'd stolen more than two hundred thousand rubles worth of jewelry and art from the Baroness spread like wildfire through the popular press. The newsrolls were full of the details of the crime, and a couple of the wire services picked up the news and spread it to several of the nearby star systems. Within twenty-four hours, the cat burglars of Cordoba were known to almost everyone on five planets who could read or listen to the news.

Jules and Yvette did not rest on their laurels, either. With their notoriety firmly established, they began a series of robberies every bit as thrilling as the first. Since there was no need to make further splash, they stayed away from the nobility and confined their burglaries to rich members of the common classes. Their take was less, but that was of no concern to them. The important factor was that the risk was also substantially lessened; after all, why should they take the chance of being caught accidentally, before they'd even begun their true job?

Speculation was rife about the identity of these ingenious criminals. It was repeatedly stressed that the thieves could not hope to dispose of their loot, since most of it was highly identifiable and the police were carefully monitoring all the known fences. That detail mattered not at all to the two SOTE agents; once they had accomplished their purpose, they intended to let the loot be found intact. Only the identities of the thieves would remain perpetually undiscovered.

In the meantime, while they spent the late night hours committing their crimes, their afternoons and early evenings were occupied in another phase of their plan. They had to become known within the local underworld and, in particular, they had to find out where and how they could make contact with someone to "disappear" when the time was ripe.

In order to maximize their contact, the two of them split up and frequented the various hangouts separately. Jules haunted several of the bars, a task he personally disliked—all DesPlainians were allergic to alcoholic beverages and, while there were other stimulants available to him, Jules hated cluttering up his body with what he considered contaminants and poisons. Still, this was considered part of his duty, and he tried to bear it with as few complaints as possible.

After a week he became one of the regulars. The same faces were in and out all the time, and from overheard bits of conversation he could tell which people were involved in which illegal activities. He struck up acquaintances with several of the more promising candidates. They were suspicious of him, at first; newcomers could always be possible police spies or informants. But Jules worked hard to allay their fears. He displayed a genuine unconcern for the details of their crimes—after all, SOTE was not a police agency, and it was not his business to arrest criminals unless their activity bordered on treason.

At length, the people of the underworld came to realize that this affable stranger was no threat to them, and that he was a new audience for all their old boasts and stories. Jules also made it clear he was in the same business, though he made no claim to being one of the now-famous cat burglars. An easy camaraderie was established, and Jules felt he would be able to make the proper connections when he had to.

Yvette, meanwhile, was making her own connections elsewhere. While Jules frequented the bars, Yvette made the rounds of the gambling casinos. Gambling was technically illegal on Cordoba, but it was so common a pastime that most law enforcement officials merely looked the other way; the casinos that stayed within respectable limits managed to thrive.

The casinos took all forms. There were some, for the very upper classes, that were located inside posh manor houses. There, amid elegant surroundings, the wealthy people of Cordoba could wager their fortunes with style and dignity. For the middle classes, the casinos usually masqueraded as private clubs or social organizations, complete with membership fees and constitutions. The style was more casual here, though the ultimate results were the same.

Those were not the places Yvette visited. Hers were the dives, the dirty back rooms, the cramped, grimy cellars that smelled more of sweat and stale dopesticks than of perfume and incense. The atmosphere was much more frenetic here, and the gambling seemed more a compulsion than a means of relaxation. Yvette could not help but compare the desperation here with the luxurious conditions she had seen at the famous casinos on Vesa. These places were less crowded than Vesa's, but the tension in them was even more tangible.

Women were not uncommon in these places, although they were usually there to hustle up a little business on their own. Yvette was a good gambler, moderately successful, and she managed to work her way into the confidence of many of the regulars. After four days of steady attendance, she was deemed good enough to be invited into some private games that went on in back rooms. The conversation there was salty, but Yvette picked up a lot more information from chance remarks than the utterers would have believed. She, too, was building a list of possible people to contact when the time came to vanish.

One day, coming out of a private poker game into the main room, she spotted her brother with his back toward her, standing in the middle of a crowd across the way. She was a little startled; this was supposed to be her turf, and Jules would not have come unless something were about to happen. Crossing quickly to him, she said, "I didn't expect to see you here."

Then the man turned around, and she saw her mistake. It was not her brother after all, but another man with the same distinctive build of a native from some high-grav world. He looked her up and down and gave her a pleasant smile. "I didn't expect to see you here, either," he said. "But I'm certainly glad I did."

Yvette gave him a thorough once-over. He was a most handsome young man, possibly in his middle thirties, with light blue eyes and sandy brown hair that curled in ringlets onto his forehead. He was dressed like a dandy, with a sleeveless U-necked jumpsuit made of black glitter-fabric and pants legs that flared at the bottom. Under this, he wore a white satin shirt with large, puffy sleeves. The shirt was open at the neck and had rows of ruffles covering the front. A waist-length black velvet cape was draped casually about his shoulders and a broad-brimmed black hat with a flat top was tilted at a cocky angle on his head. Tucked into the hat's brim on the right side was a large red rose.

"Excuse me," Yvette stammered, embarrassed. "From the back, I mistook you for my brother Jaro."

The man doffed his hat and swept it across the front of his chest as part of a courtly bow. "You flatter me, gospozha. Any man related to you would have to be far better looking than I. If I may be of any use to you instead of him, my name is Pias Nav, at your service."

The excess of gallantry might have seemed ludicrous

55

in anyone else, but in this young man it seemed to complement and complete his personality. Although there were some snickers from the back of the room at such elegant behavior in such a seamy setting, Pias Nav's innate dignity overcame any possible embarrassment.

"Thank you, gospodin, for your offer, but it really isn't necessary. My name is Yarmilla, by the way—Yarmilla Dubcek."

"I am honored." He took her hand and touched it lightly to his lips as though she were a grand duchess instead of—supposedly—a common gambler.

Yvette did not know quite what to make of this earnest young man—but she did know that she had an appointment to meet her brother very shortly back in his hotel room. She could not afford to stand here and allow herself to be charmed by this handsome stranger. Reluctantly she moved away and said, "It has been pleasant meeting you, even under these awkward circumstances. But right now I really must go and meet my brother. He gets very angry when I keep him waiting."

"As would I, gospozha, as would I. What man could bear the thought of your not being there? I let you go with the greatest of regret and the greatest wish for your happiness. Until we meet again, if we ever do." And again, he swept his arm in another grand gesture.

Yvette left the casino, a very bemused woman indeed.

CHAPTER 5

The Disappearance of Jaroslav and Yarmilla

"It's a good thing we weren't born needing money," Yvette commented. "With our skills, we could have been the scourges of the spaceways."

She stood with her hands on her hips in front of the loot they had collected on their burglaries over the past ten days. It had been arranged neatly into two stacks, with jewelry on one side and art objects on the other, and stored in the food locker in an abandoned meat-packing plant. They had not attempted to dispose of it in any way; once their assignment was over, the police would be informed of its whereabouts and it would be redistributed among its owners. But in the meantime, it was as safe here as anywhere.

"Yes, but all good things must come to an end, to coin a phrase," her brother said. "Our criminal career is about to be behind us. It's time to move on to the real job."

"*C'est vrai.* It'll be nice to be able to look at myself respectfully in the mirror again."

Jules went outside to a public vidicom booth and dialed the number for the main Avila police station. "Hello," he said in a growly voice that was not remotely like his own, "I've got some information about those two cat burglars."

"If you'll hold on just a minute, gospodin," said a

57

female voice, "I'll connect you with the détectives in charge of that investigation."

"No!" Jules croaked vehemently. "I'll tell you, now, or I don't talk to anyone." The girl at the other end of the line was clever; if she could have persuaded him to hold the line open, the call would be traced back to this number. Jules wanted his call to be completely anonymous.

"Very well, gospodin, I'll take the message." The woman would be signaling someone in her department to trace the call anyway, but Jules didn't care about that. By the time they could even get started, he would be finished.

"Look for a man and a woman named Jaroslav and Yarmilla Dubcek. They're brother and sister, I believe, and they're staying at the Androvoy Hotel." Without further ado he cut off the line. *Let them try to trace that,* he thought smugly.

The d'Alemberts could have predicted quite accurately the events that would transpire next. Within fifteen minutes, several squads of police would converge on the Androvoy Hotel. They would indeed find that Jaroslav and Yarmilla Dubcek were registered in adjoining rooms on the second floor, and that they were frequently out to all hours of the night. Proceeding up to the rooms, they would discover that the suspects were nowhere around, but there would be plenty of equipment—ropes, grippers, wire cutters, electrical apparatus—to indicate that the Dubceks were indeed the cat burglars. No trace would be found of the loot they had taken—nor would there be any clear fingerprints to use as identification. The two agents had been very careful on that point, because they wanted to leave no permanent traces of themselves here.

With that much to go on, the police search would begin in earnest. Hotel staff and guests would be ques-

58

tioned for any information they could give concerning the two strangers. In a relatively short time a description of the fugitive pair would be flashed to police stations all over the planet, and from there the information would be disseminated to individual officers. Within two or three hours, the d'Alemberts, alias Dubceks, would be the two most wanted people on the entire planet.

This, they knew, was the chanciest part of their entire plan. They had to count on the contacts they had made to help them reach the agents for the conspiracy. Cordoba had been chosen specifically because more criminals had vanished from here than from any other world—but that did not mean lightning would strike again. The conspiracy normally took native criminals with long past histories; the d'Alemberts were hoping that their recent record was spectacular enough to make them worthy prospects.

If they could not get in touch with the conspiracy, they'd find themselves in serious trouble. They would be the subjects of a massive manhunt, the likes of which this planet had never before seen. All ships taking off, including their own, would be thoroughly searched. Just giving back what they'd stolen would not be any excuse for having taken it in the first place, and the hunt for them would continue. Should they be caught, they dared not break their covers and reveal their true identities—it would nullify their future usefulness to the Service. They'd be forced to serve their time in prison like any other criminals.

The plan would just have to succeed. They had no other option.

They waited for about three hours, so that news about the Dubceks would begin filtering down through the ranks of the underworld. Then, when they were certain people would know about their plight, they began calling their respective contacts, pleading for help.

"The offs are closing in," they would say when they reached one of their newfound friends. "I need somewhere to hide, fast. Can you help me?"

The reply, if there was one, was usually a quick no; most of the time, the connection was simply broken with no response at all. *You sure learn in a hurry who your friends are,* Yvette thought after her sixth call had ended in a discouragingly negative response.

Finally, Jules hit paydirt. The man at the other end of the line was silent for a minute, then said in slow, careful tones, "There *might* be a way. I've heard of some people who specialize in that sort of thing. What's it worth to you to find out?"

"Five thousand rubles."

"Make it ten." The guy at the other end knew he had the upper hand, and was prepared to make the most of it.

Jules pretended to hesitate and consider. *"Khorosho,* you've got a deal. How quickly can you find out for me?"

"It might take an hour or two. Do you have a number where I can reach you?"

Jules gave a bitter laugh. "No, circumstances compel me to remain mobile at this time. Why don't I call you back at this number in, say, three hours? Will that do?"

"Smooth." The man clicked off, and Jules went to inform his sister that their all-important connection was on the verge of being made.

That left them only with the problem of how to spend the intervening time without getting caught. Retreating to public 'freshers, each of them put on a wig and enough makeup to disguise their faces from recognition on casual scrutiny. Then they went to a local amusement park, taking advantage of the crowds to hide themselves and have a few moments of relaxation before they had to return to work. The thrilling rides, the cries of the barkers and the smells of concession-stand food reminded them very much of the midway of their own beloved Circus. Every so often, one or the other of them would stop dead and let the atmosphere of the place wash over him. The other would stand patiently by and wait until the rapture had passed, and then the two would move on without a word being spoken. Each knew what the other felt. The Circus had been their entire life for more than twenty-five years; even their loyalty and duty to the Empire could not fill the emotional void that leaving the Circus had imparted.

At last their time at the park drew to a close. The respite was a brief one, and now they would have to go back to the dangers of their work. Even as they walked toward the front gate, Yvette reached over and squeezed Jules's hand abruptly, whispering a single word: "Rube."

The abbreviated version of the old circus battle cry "Hey Rube!" brought Jules instantly to attention, though outwardly he continued to appear relaxed. Glancing casually in the direction his sister's eyes indicated, he saw a policeman in uniform walking slowly toward them. The man did not have a weapon drawn and seemed slightly hesitant, which was a positive sign. He had probably been told to look for anyone with a build that indicated high gravity origins. Even though the d'Alemberts had deliberately worn loose-fitting clothing and had changed their faces slightly, they were still close enough to the description of the wanted burglars to arouse suspicion in this officer. He was coming over to check them out more closely—something they could not afford at this stage of the game.

"I copy," Jules whispered back. "We split, no panic unless called for. Rendezvous Site B."

"Smooth."

Quite casually, the two began to drift apart, each walking perpendicular to the other's path until they were separated by more than thirty meters. At this point, the policeman realized what they were doing and his suspicions doubled. Without a partner to help him, he decided to go after Jules and leave Yvette alone. He began walking faster. Jules, noticing this, also began walking faster, so that the gap between himself and the officer remained constant. Every time the policeman increased his pace slightly, Jules did likewise.

Finally the policeman tired of this game. "Wait up, you!" he called out to Jules. "I'd like to talk to you."

Obligingly, Jules halted. He turned to face the officer, his face a mask of utter innocence. Then, after putting the policeman momentarily off his guard, he made his move. From a dead stop, he suddenly raced off toward a group of sheds at a speed that left the officer sputtering with amazement. It took a full two seconds for that worthy to even think about drawing his stungun, by which time Jules was well out of range. The innocent bystanders wandering through the scene would have made random shooting hazardous in any event. There was nothing the policeman could do except try to run after his suspect.

Jules had little difficulty putting distance between himself and his pursuer. With his special athletic training and the inborn speed of a son of DesPlaines, he constantly increased his lead, dodging between and around groups of startled spectators. The policeman managed to keep him in sight, but that was about all.

Finally Jules made it to the sheds and ducked behind them. For one brief moment he would be out of the lawman's viewing range. Two meters away was the outer wall of the amusement park, barely three meters high—an easy leap for a man with Jules's abilities. But

Jules did not take that avenue of escape. Once the policeman knew that Jules had fled that way, he would call in to headquarters and the area surrounding the park would be cordoned off for kilometers around. He might be able to slip through such a blockade, but it would be time consuming and risky.

Instead, he elected to jump to the roof of the shed. He made it in a single easy leap, then waited, crouched, for his pursuer to appear.

The man rounded the corner at top speed, gun drawn. He saw the wall and hesitated, thinking that his suspect must surely have gone over it already. While he stood there hesitating, Jules dropped on him from the rooftop. The impact of his hundred-kilo body caused the gun to fly out of the policeman's hand. Jules used his forward momentum to roll in the appropriate direction. He swooped up the stunner, rose to his feet, checked the gun's setting—it was on three—and fired, all in one continuous motion.

With the officer now definitely unconscious for twenty minutes, and too groggy to report for perhaps another ten, Jules took a slight running start and leaped easily over the fence. In half an hour, he could be so far away from here that no cordon would be successful—and the police would know it. They would have to keep their attention dispersed throughout the city—which was fine with Jules. In the meantime, he had a call to make, and it was already ten minutes overdue.

"What kept you?" said his contact when Jules finally got to a vidicom booth and placed the call. "I don't like to be kept waiting."

"And I don't like being caught," Jules retorted angrily. "In case you don't know it, every off in the city is looking for me. Have you got what I want?"

"It's all set. That's for you and your sister, right?"

"Right."

"It'll cost you."

"How much?"

"Fifty thousand rubles."

"That's not too bad, I guess, if they can deliver the goods."

"That's apiece."

Jules feigned shock. "That's robbery. I'll pay forty each."

The man at the other end of the line smiled a greasy smile. "You ain't in no position to bargain, *tovarishch*. My contact says it's an even hundred for the both of you or no deal. Take it or leave it."

"You're right, I have no choice. *Khorosho,* what are the details?"

"You're to get all your worldly possessions together in one small bundle. All dealings from here on are strictly cash, so you'd better have a lot of it. On top of the hundred thou for him and the ten for me, he says to plan on living expenses for several years. You're going to be gone a long time, *tovarishch,* but it's necessary to clean your trail."

"Understood."

The man gave Jules the address of a warehouse on the south side of the city. "You and your sister are to be there in ninety minutes, no later. If you're not there, you've missed the ship and no one'll listen to your story again. Copy?"

"Copy," said Jules. The other man nodded and the line went dead. Jules felt exhilarated—the plan had worked, and they were now on the road Helena had probably taken.

Rendezvous Site B was a specific group of bushes in the plaza across from one of Avila's major hotels. Yvette was waiting for him as he strolled past, and she took his arm like a long lost sweetheart. "You sure took your time getting here," she said. "I had to wrestle a couple of squirrellike things for the right to stay there."

"I may be slow, but I get results." Jules told her about his conversation, and what they were supposed to do.

Yvette gave a low whistle. "Demanding lot, aren't they? All they want is everything we've got, immediately. What if it's a trap? What if they deliberately lure fugitives into their lair with a promise of sanctuary, kill them, take everything they have—which could be a tidy sum, considering some of their clients—and then dispose of the bodies? It would be a sweet racket—and there'd be absolutely no one to blow the whistle on them."

"Whatever their game is, we'll have to find it out eventually. This has got to be the route Helena went; if there's murder involved, it's best that we learn about it now. I'm not recommending that we walk in there like lambs to the slaughter. But," he added, looking at his watch, "if we don't walk in there soon, we might as well not go at all."

They walked quickly to a garage where they had previously parked a rented car. The suitcase in the trunk contained a couple changes of clothing for each of them and five hundred thousand rubles in cash. The Circus maintained master bank accounts on every planet it visited, and they were able to tap into this fund for "incidental" expenses. So top secret was their work that they were not even on SOTE's payroll. The Emperor saw to it that the Circus's taxes were secretly rebated—and so large was this sum that it was sufficient to bankroll any operations the d'Alemberts saw fit to perform.

The two agents counted out a hundred and ten thousand rubles in cash and stashed it in Yvette's purse; the rest was put back into the suitcase for future use. Quickly then, for the deadline was almost upon them, they drove to a spot three blocks away from the designated warehouse and walked the rest of the way, with Jules carrying the suitcase casually in his left hand. His right hand stayed near his pocket where he had a mini-stunner hidden; Yvette's mini was already cached in the palm of her hand. Each agent was prepared for any trouble that might arise.

They approached the warehouse cautiously. There was only one door that they could spot, and they didn't have the time to look for alternative means of access. The door was slightly ajar and they had to squeeze in one at a time, fully aware that several blasters would probably be trained on them each step of the way from now on.

The ceiling of the warehouse towered more than fifteen meters above their heads, and the enormous room stretched for perhaps two hundred meters in front of them. Large boxes and heavy crates were stacked efficiently in rows, with aisles wide enough to permit a forklift to travel with ease. There was the smell of sawdust in the air, a clean, woodsy scent.

Jules and Yvette started walking down the center aisle slowly, mindful of a possible ambush. As they approached one intersection, Jules's contact man stepped out in front of them from behind some crates. He was apparently unarmed.

"Glad to see you could make it," he said. "I presume you have my ten thousand."

Yvette reached into her purse and fished out the appropriate bundle. "Here you are."

The man took the stack of bills and counted it with experienced rapidity. "*Khorosho*," he announced when he'd finished. "It's been a pleasure doing business with you. I now turn you over to Gospodin Kharmahn, who will handle your affairs the rest of the way."

As he spoke, another man emerged from a side aisle one intersection further up. Kharmahn was of average height and weight, with red hair and beard. A long white scar twisted its way down the left side of his face from temple to lips, and his left eye seemed larger and redder than his right. He walked with the faintest trace of a limp in his left leg. He too appeared unarmed, but the d'Alemberts guessed that he had some confederates backing him up who would be armed to the teeth.

"Good afternoon, comrades. I trust our mutual friend has explained the details of our transaction." He nodded his head to indicate Jules's contact, who was even now disappearing out the door with his money.

The two agents walked forward slowly toward Kharmahn. "Somewhat," Jules answered. "He was quite adamant about the price."

"It's our standard," Kharmahn shrugged. "You are being charged no more nor less than anyone else who has used our services. I presume that suitcase contains enough money to last you for a while. You will be traveling to a place of temporary retirement, and you'll be forced to live off of your previous earnings."

"We'll manage," Jules said cagily.

"*Khorosho.* Then if I can have your payment, we can proceed."

As before, Yvette reached into her purse and produced the desired amount. Kharmahn took the bundle casually and did not bother to count it. "I know you won't cheat us," he said. "Your lives will be in our hands for quite some while, and that would not be to your benefit. Now, would you come this way, please?"

Kharman led them down one row of crates and stopped before a large leaden one that was marked in bright red letters:

DANGER
FISSIONABLE MATERIALS
RADIOACTIVE

Walking right up to the crate, Kharmahn pressed an almost invisible stud on the side. One metal side swung open to reveal a smaller lead box inside, just barely big enough for two people.

"Those will be your travel accommodations, I'm afraid. Not luxurious, but you'll only be in there a maximum of three hours. Oxygen masks will of course be provided. Once you're sealed in, we do indeed fill the rest of the crate with radioactive material, to pass inspection at the spaceport. Don't worry, your own private container is more than sufficiently shielded to protect you from the hazards. It's just that we've found the authorities are a little more willing to pass on fissionable material with a minimum of inspection—and, of course, with all the radioactivity inside and shielding around it, they couldn't begin to X-ray it. Once your ship has safely taken off, you will be decanted, as it were, and given better quarters until you reach your ultimate destination. Please get in now."

The d'Alemberts climbed into the tiny box with their suitcase and adjusted the oxygen masks about their faces. Room within the compartment was at a premium, and both DesPlainians found themselves wishing they had learned to be contortionists like some of their other relatives in the Circus. Three hours of this was bound to be a grueling ordeal.

As soon as their crate was closed up, they could feel themselves being moved to another location—presumably to add the fissionable material around them. Their compartment was pretty thoroughly soundproofed so they felt, rather than heard, the vibration of the loading. Then they were moved again to what apparently was the back of a truck for, after being at rest for half an hour, there was a constant jostling movement that indicated they were being driven somewhere. Hopefully, their destination was the spaceport.

There was still, in the back of their minds, the fear that this might be some sort of elaborate trap. They were no longer worried that their box would be simply dumped in the ocean—Kharmahn would never have let them take the suitcase inside with them if he intended that—but they were only too aware of how dependent they were on those oxygen masks. All Kharmahn had to do was pump poison gas in to kill them effortlessly, then open up the crate and take their money.

They had to have faith in their hypothesis that the cabel behind these disappearances had further plans for the criminal talent they were assembling, and that their clients would be more use to them alive than dead. As time dragged by and the bumpy ride in the truck continued, that hypothesis looked more and more likely. If Kharmahn had intended to kill the d'Alemberts, he would have done so quickly and disposed of them. The fact that they were being taken for a long ride was an indication that he had been smooth with them.

After an hour the jostling ride stopped. Suddenly their crate was hoisted roughly into the air and they were bounced around inside their tiny compartment. The bruises they received only added to the torment of their already cramped muscles. Their crate was set down again with a harsh bump, and there they sat for half an hour. Then the lifting and setting process was repeated another time. The agents were just coming to the conclusion that this was not so much an escape as a series of carefully designed tortures when they felt a new force suddenly pressing them down hard against the floor of their chamber. This, at least, was a very familiar feeling—the acceleration of a spaceship taking off. The three gees of acceleration would have felt good to them under normal circumstances but, cramped as they were, it only added to their discomfort.

When the acceleration finally ended, they experienced the opposite sensation—zero gee. The floating feeling eased the pain in their limbs a little, but not too much.

Finally, after what seemed like an eternity of confinement, they could feel the material around them being unloaded. Then their box opened and light streamed in on them, blinding after so long a period in darkness. They blinked furiously, squinting against the light, and eventually they could see the silhouettes of three men standing before them. Rough hands reached in and grabbed their arms, yanking them ungently out of their compartment.

"Welcome aboard the *Linnea Rose*," said one harsh voice. "You're on your way to Sanctuary."

CHAPTER 6

Flight to Sanctuary

With their bodies aching from the abuse of their confinement, the d'Alemberts climbed gratefully out of their hiding place. They were in the hold of what was obviously a cargo ship, surrounded by scores of other boxes and crates much like their own.

"Do all those boxes have people in them?" Jules asked as he began doing some freefall exercises to limber up his muscles once again. Yvette, too, was stretching herself out full length and twisting her body in odd ways to get the kinks out of her system.

"Nah, we only take a few per trip," volunteered one of the men who'd unpacked them. "Don't have room for more than that. Come on, I'll show you to your quarters."

He swam off toward the "ceiling" of the room, its forward wall while the ship was in motion. Jules and Yvette, their bodies still sore but at least functioning, swam after him. A passenger ship would have been under ultragrav for the convenience of its more planet-bound passengers, but a cargo ship could not afford that luxury. The crewmen here learned to handle themselves in freefall or else they found other means of employment.

The crewman led them down one corridor to a pair of plain metal doors. The two adjoining rooms were identical in their stark simplicity: a zero-gee hammock stretched along one wall, a small set of drawers built into the wall for holding personal items and a personal freefall 'fresher unit set in one corner. The walls were bare metal, gray and cold.

"I suppose it's an improvement over the box we just got out of," Yvette commented. "But not much."

"You'd think fifty thousand rubles apiece would go a lot further than this," Jules added.

"Quit grumbling. You're paying for our service, not for the accommodations," the crewman said. "It'd be harder getting you offworld on a cruise ship. You'll get better quarters when you're living on Sanctuary. In the meantime, be glad you're here. Dinner'll be in two hours. Mess hall's up forward." His welcoming duties done, he left to return to his regular chores.

"Well, cramped as it is it's still better than a prison cell," Yvette said. As she talked, she reached over and touched her brother lightly on the shoulder. Her fingers tapped out a brief coded message: *The room's probably bugged.*

Jules gave a slight nod. It would be difficult for them to find anyplace aboard this ship where they could have a free conversation. They dared not expose the fact that they were infiltrators while they were in such controlled enemy territory.

"I think you're right," he said aloud. "Personally, I want to stretch out and take a nap after all that time in the box."

And he meant it. The day's activities had taken their toll; even the supernormal stamina of the d'Alemberts could be overtaxed, and today had been an exceptionally busy one. He and his sister split up, then, to get a bit of rest before dinner.

Feeling a little more refreshed, the agents met two hours later and swam together toward the front of the ship. After a short period of exploration, they found a crewman who directed them to the mess hall. By the time they got there, nearly everyone else aboard ship had already assembled.

The *Linnea Rose* had a crew of twenty-one and was carrying three passengers in addition to themselves. The others were no doubt along for the same reasons that the d'Alemberts were—they had purchased tickets to Sanctuary to escape the consequences of their crimes.

As Yvette scanned the rows of faces, she was startled to see one she recognized. It was the gambler she had met on Cordoba, the dandy from the high-grav planet whom she'd mistaken for Jules. She searched her memory frantically and after a moment came up with the name that went with the face: Pias Nav.

The gambler was dressed as grandly as before, though a bit more practically for a zero-gee environment. He was *sans chapeau* and wearing a full black jumpsuit with no cape. On the left shoulder of his garment was an artificial red rose; the soft cloth of its petals flowed gently in the air each time he moved. He caught sight of Yvette at almost the same moment she spotted him, and his face lit up with delight.

"Gospozha Dubcek!" he called loudly. All heads in the room swiveled, either to him or to the object of his attention. Pias Nav went on, oblivious to the stares. "What an unexpected pleasure running into you again. I'd been told there was a lady aboard ship, but I hadn't realized it would be you. And that must be your brother. Please do come over here by me. I insist."

Yvette smiled and started in his direction. Jules followed after her, perplexed. "Who is he?" Jules whispered as they swam down the center of the mess hall.

"He's the guy I mistook for you once at the casino. I told you about him."

Jules looked Pias Nav over from top to bottom with a

disapproving glare. "I don't see how you could have made that mistake. I'm much more handsome than he is."

Yvette gave a short laugh. "And much more prejudiced. I think he's charming."

"He's also some kind of big-time crook, or he wouldn't be here," Jules cautioned. "Keep that in mind."

They floated over and steadied themselves beside the flamboyant gambler. "I would bow, milady, but that doesn't work too well in freefall," Nav apologized. "But if I might kiss your hand as a token of my esteem—"

"Of course," Yvette offered her hand and Nav touched it to his lips as elegantly as though he were at a ball at the Imperial Court itself.

Jules floated by himself a short distance away, muttering something under his breath about "damned foppish showoffs." Then, so he wouldn't feel so useless, he went to the food dispenser and got the platters for Yvette and himself and brought them back to where his sister was still engrossed by Nav.

The food was typical space fare, hardly exciting. There was some clear broth in a squeeze bottle as soup; a globe containing bite-sized squares of protein paste that had been made to resemble cooked meat; and three more squeeze tubes containing creamed vegetables, hot coffee and a custardy dessert, respectively.

"Well, we hardly have to worry about spoiling ourselves on this," Jules commented as he handed his sister her meal.

"Never mind, milady," said Nav. "With you beside me, even the simplest repast is a banquet beyond compare."

I think I'm going to throw up, Jules thought, but kept his opinion of the gambler's loquacity very much to himself. He sucked on his broth and vegetables and chewed the protein squares in silence.

In some ways, though, Nav's blather was proving very useful. A natural-born busybody, he had already learned a great deal about their fellow passengers. "That fellow over there," he said, indicating a lean, middle-aged man with rapidly thinning hair and squinted eyes, "is the former accountant for the Earl of Arabolia. It is supposed that he managed to embezzle nearly two million rubles before vacating his post in somewhat of a hurry; he refuses to quote exact figures, though. And our other companion is Rowe Carnery, who has pirated ships successfully from more than a score of planets."

Yvette thought she detected a slight change in Nav's voice when he talked about Carnery—a little bit less lightness, a darker undertone. *There's something strange between Nav and Carnery,* her instincts told her, although she had no real evidence on which to base that assumption.

Still, she gave Carnery a very thorough scrutiny. The man was big, just under two meters tall and easily massing a hundred and ten kilos. His black hair was cut close to his scalp, and his bushy eyebrows grew together to make one dark line across the bottom of his forehead. He had a two-day growth of stubble on his face and a nose that had been broken several times in the past. His deep-set dark eyes brooded over some hidden horrors that only he could see. *Definitely not the sort of character to take on a picnic,* Yvette decided. *I wonder what the connection is between him and Nav.*

She told Nav the story about herself and her brother, about their being the famed cat burglars, and he was duly impressed. "What about yourself?" she asked when she'd finished. "What did you do to merit this trip to Sanctuary?"

"Ah, compared to such illustrious company my sins are positively puny," said Nav with a flourish. "I am, by trade, a gambler, and I gambled entirely too well to suit certain casino owners back on Cordoba. After I had won several hundred thousand rubles from a few of them, they pooled their resources in thinking up methods to discourage me. The latest method involved sending a couple of their bouncers to rough me up. In trying to defend myself, one of the men ended up dead, so they took that opportunity to frame me for murder. This trip seemed a more convenient alternative than explaining the story to the local police."

"You don't look like a very experienced fighter to me," Jules commented icily.

"Indeed I'm not," Nav agreed with a cheery smile. "There are times when most of my energies are directed at preventing violence. But, as I'm sure you know, these people from the lighter gravity planets can sometimes move too slowly for their own good."

This turn in the conversation gave Yvette a perfect chance to ask, "Where are you from, by the way? You don't have a DesPlainian accent, and you're obviously not from Purity. There aren't too many high-grav worlds."

"Indeed there aren't," Nav smiled. "I happen to be from Newforest."

Yvette's eyes widened just a trifle. Newforest was the so called Lost Colony that had been a myth for centuries until finally discovered just fifty years ago. In the early twenty-first century, a group of some two dozen small ships filled with dissident gypsies and "tinkers" took off from England to avoid the purges that were then sweeping Earth. All contact was broken and, by the official formation of the Empire of Earth in 2225, it was generally assumed that the ships had either been lost in an uncharted sector of space or else had landed

76

on an inhospitable world where no survivors were left.

But there were strange occurrences. Every so often, a spaceship would set down on a rural planet. The captain and crew would claim to be inhabitants of a world called Newforest, and that they were descendants of the people from those lost ships. Eventually these Newforesters took on mythic proportions. About all that was known about them was that they came from a high-grav planet whose location they kept totally secret.

After some elaborate detective work on the part of the Service of the Empire, the actual location of Newforest was deduced. The planet circled close to a red star so small and faint that it was almost totally ignored in galactic surveys. The population of Newforest had been very uncertain about the Empire, remembering the purges that had driven them off Earth in the first place. But when a fleet of twenty-five imperial battlecruisers appeared in their skies demanding that they pledge their loyalty to the Empire or be obliterated, they had no choice but to join Earth's system of government.

The affair had caused a sensation five decades ago, but since then things had settled down. Newforest, a world with two and a half times the surface gravity of Earth, turned out to be a very quiet, bucolic place. Its people for the most part minded their own business and caused little trouble. Citizens from Newforest—as did citizens from all heavy-grav worlds—traveled seldom because of the discomfort of constantly adjusting to weaker gravitational systems. Consequently, Newforest was known more for its exotic past than for its commonplace present.

"I've never met anyone from Newforest before," Yvette said, quite honestly. "What's it like there?"

Given a prompting like that, the verbose gambler could elaborate for hours. He began telling Yvette, in his usual elegant terms, what life was like under a dim red sun. He described the brilliant crimson foliage and the fascinating native animals. He told her of some of the customs that had developed on the planet during its centuries of isolation from the rest of humanity, and what life might be like for a typical Newforester. So eloquent was his style that Yvette floated and listened to him, entranced.

Jules, meanwhile, had finished his dinner and was feeling terribly bored. His sister was devoting all her attention to that jackdandle beside her, and Nav was playing to his audience like a master musician. The few remarks Jules made were lightly passed over as inconsequential, making him feel as useless as wheels on a starship. Finally tired of floating idly by while the other two chattered, he excused himself and left the mess hall. His departure was barely noticed.

Needing something better to do than stretch out in his room and brood over Yvette's preoccupation with that garrulous wastrel, Jules decided to explore the ship. Swimming up and down the passageways, he soon learned the locations of the crew's quarters, the galley, the recycling stations, the cargo holds and the officers' lounge. That last place, he was informed in haughty tones by the officer in there at the time, was completely off limits to him. As a passenger, he apparently was expected to stay mostly in his own cabin except for meals—a routine that could become very boring indeed.

During his roving, though, he did find something extremely useful. It was a hatch that he almost missed at first glance and, opening it, he discovered a small storeroom for oxygen tanks and safety equipment. It had the musty smell of a place that was seldom used—and it was almost certain to be free of electronic bugs. This would be a place where he and Yvette could come and share their ideas in complete privacy—something they had been hoping to find. Excited by his discovery, he went back to their adjoining rooms to tell Yvette. She wasn't back from dinner yet, so he went to his own room to sulk until she returned.

One hour and forty-three minutes later—he had kept very careful track of the time—he heard voices out in the corridor. Opening his door a crack, he peeked out to see exactly what was going on. There was Yvette locked tightly in an embrace with her new acquaintance. Out of embarrassment, Jules averted his eyes. The kiss seemed to last forever; had it been practical in free-fall Jules would have been tapping his foot with impatience. At last Nav left and Yvette slipped into her room alone.

Jules swam quietly over and rapped lightly on her door. She opened it and was about to greet him, but he put his finger to his lips, indicating he wanted silence. Then he beckoned her to follow him and willingly she did so.

He took her to the storeroom he'd found. "I think we'll be able to talk privately here," he said. "I can't imagine anyone in his right mind bugging a place like this."

"Perfect," Yvette said.

Without further preamble, Jules said, "I think you ought to watch yourself with that smooth-talking Newforester. I don't like it."

"Why? Just because he's charming and amusing and knows how to treat a lady with respect?"

"He's a crook, and we can't afford to get ourselves romantically entangled with people like that. Not in our line of work."

Yvette looked at him with narrowed eyes. *"Mon Dieu,* my brother is a prude! I wouldn't have believed it!" She tried to make light of the situation, but stopped when she saw how serious he was. "Listen, he's not a real crook. He's a professional gambler, which is legal on a large number of planets. The only reason he's here is because he got involved in a situation he couldn't get out of by himself. That hardly makes him Galactic Enemy Number One."

"You believe his story, then?"

"For the time being. He's given me no cause not to."

"He's an admitted murderer."

"So are we, *mon cher frère,* so are we. We've had to kill at times, both in self-defense and for the good of the Empire. I won't condemn him solely on those grounds."

Jules slapped his left palm with his right fist. "There's something not right about him, Evie. That's all I can say right now. Something about his story just doesn't lie smooth. He's not being completely honest with us."

"I'll tell you what," Yvette said, trying to assuage her brother's ruffled feelings. "You get me some proof and then I'll believe you. I trust your feelings when you say he's not being honest—but I ask you to trust mine that I know he's a good man."

Jules grimaced. *"Khorosho,* you've got a deal. But I warn you, I'm really going to be looking closely at him."

"Knowing you," Yvette smiled, "I wouldn't expect it any other way."

At breakfast the next day, Pias Nav was still his same, cheerful self, charming Yvette and disgusting Jules with his excessive gallantry. But at lunchtime the gambler did not show up in the mess hall when everyone else did. This made Jules suspicious; on a ship where meals were the only social activity permitted, missing one was not something a person would do casually. Jules wolfed down his food and made an excuse to leave early; this was something that needed looking into.

He swam down the corridors to what he'd been told was Nav's room, but there was no answer to his knock. On a hunch he went back to his and Yvette's rooms, half expecting to find the Newforester rifling through them. But they were both untouched. Perplexed now, he wandered the hallways silently, wondering where the man could be and what he was up to.

Finally he heard a faint noise. A door on his left was slightly ajar—it was the door, he had learned earlier, to Rowe Carnery's cabin. Approaching it slowly, he put his eye up to the crack and looked in. There was Nav, fishing neatly through the drawers of the built-in bureau. He would take out one article of clothing, look through it and, not finding what he was looking for, set it aside and repeat the process. Finally he found something that interested him—a large round medallion on a silver chain. Nav held it up to the light and examined it closely for a minute, then clenched his fist around it. The expression on his face changed to one of pure hatred, with a murderous glint in the eyes that sent an involuntary chill down Jules's spine. *I don't care what Evie thinks, that's no innocent lamb there,* Jules thought. *I'd hate to run afoul of anyone who can look like that.*

After almost a minute, Nav's normal expression of blandness returned. Very carefully he put the medallion back exactly where he'd found it, and restacked the clothing in the drawers so neatly that Carnery would never guess it had been touched.

This is my cue to leave, Jules decided. *I don't want him to know I've been spying on him.* He managed to swim quickly down the corridor and out of sight before Nav emerged once more from the room and swam off in the opposite direction toward the mess hall.

Later that evening, as Jules and Yvette were swimming down the corridor together toward dinner, Jules

81

took his sister aside into their storeroom. "Would you be able to keep your friend occupied for an hour or two after supper? I'd like to search his cabin."

"Only an hour or two?" There was a hint of a twinkle in Yvette's eyes. "Smooth, that shouldn't be any problem. I'll bet you don't find anything, though."

"I have to check anyhow." Jules decided not to tell her yet about what he'd seen earlier; he wanted to present her with a complete package of evidence all at one time.

Again, Jules ate quickly and slipped away from the mess hall without being noticed. Pias Nav was entirely too wrapped up with Yvette to bother much about her brother. With singleminded determination, Jules swam down the halls until he came to the gambler's cabin.

The door was locked, but the mechanism was an extremely simple one and Jules—with his extensive training and experience in such matters—had little trouble persuading it to open for him. The interior of the cabin was much like his own, which meant there would be relatively few places to search. If the pattern was the same in Nav's case, he hadn't had much time to pack before coming here, so there wouldn't be much to search through. Still, Jules hoped to find some clue that would tell him more about this mysterious Newforester.

Despite the fact that he'd been rushed, Nav had taken an extraordinary amount of jewelry with him—mostly rings and pins, with a couple of ornate pendants. There were several different changes of clothing and large stacks of cash. Interestingly there were no dice, cards or other appurtenances of the gambler's trade; that was odd, though hardly condemnatory.

Jules was just about to close one drawer in disgust and write this foray off as a total loss when a single detail caught his eye. Reaching into a stack of clothing, he pulled out a neatly folded handkerchief with the initials "PB" daintily embroidered at one corner.

Either he steals other people's handkerchiefs, Jules mused, *or else "Pias Nav" is not the name he always goes by. I wonder what Evie would have to say about that.*

Tucking the handkerchief back where he'd found it, Jules gave the cabin another quick glance to make sure he had overlooked nothing, then left as stealthily as he had entered—making sure to lock the door behind him again as he went out.

There was nothing definite yet that he could present to Yvette as a case against the Newforester. The rifling of Carnery's cabin and the handkerchief with the different initials were reasons for suspicion but not damning evidence. Pias Nav was not the simple gambler he pretended to be, of that Jules was sure now. But the full story behind this mystery still required elucidation.

Pias Nav, decided Jules, *is going to require a hell of a lot closer inspection.*

CHAPTER 7

Settling In

The flight from Cordoba to Sanctuary lasted four more days. During that time, although Jules kept a very careful watch on Nav's behavior, the Newforester did nothing further that was the least bit strange. Nav spent an increasing amount of time in Yvette's company, and Yvette was not complaining at all. She actually seemed to enjoy the gallant flirtatiousness that so sickened Jules, and there were a couple of times when Jules noticed his sister gazing at Nav with a certain wistfulness in her eyes. He wondered what it all could mean.

Had he been able to step out of his skin and view his own behavior a little more dispassionately, he would have realized exactly what it meant. That same faraway look frequently was in his own eyes when he was with his fiancée, Yvonne Roumenier. The simple fact was that Yvette was falling in love with this smooth-talking stranger from the gypsy world.

Being shut out of his sister's universe so thoroughly, Jules tried to keep his mind on business. He struck up casual acquaintances with the other two passengers; but nothing much came out of them. Pasqual Ortiz, the embezzler, was a null sort of person, the type one could easily forget while standing right next to him. Aside from his apparent skill at juggling other people's funds, he had few talents to recommend him. Rowe Carnery, on the other hand, was a man who had led too exciting a life and refused to talk about it. He disliked being approached, and would speak in grunts or brief sentences at best. Jules could tell that there was a streak of violence in the man lying close to the surface, and he was loathe to do anything to bring it out—nothing would be accomplished at this point by antagonizing their fellow refugees from justice.

Jules tried making friends with the crew of the *Linnea Rose,* but found them almost as uncommunicative as Carnery. They had their jobs to do and, even when Jules—out of boredom more than anything else—pitched in and helped, they refused to talk about more than trivial matters. In particular he could get no information at all concerning their destination. Either the crew knew nothing about Sanctuary or they were under strict orders not to discuss it.

Consequently Jules spent most of his time alone in his cabin, resenting Yvette's growing affection for Nav and concocting elaborate and diabolical explanations for the Newforester's enigmatic behavior.

They were given exactly ten minutes' warning that the ship was about to break out of subspace above the surface of Sanctuary. They strapped themselves into their hammocks and experienced the familiar flickering of reality that marked the transition between normal and subetheric space. Then, in two more hours, they were going through the braking procedure as the *Linnea Rose* screamed down through the planetary atmosphere and settled gently on the spaceport field.

Then the passengers were herded out of the ship and into a long, low white building. There, under a large sign that read "Welcome to Sanctuary," their luggage was opened and searched thoroughly before their eyes, so there could be no charges of theft later. Their bodies were frisked, too, for any trace of weapons. "We don't like having guns loose on Sanctuary," one guard ex-

85

plained. "We prefer to keep it peaceful. You shouldn't need them here, anyhow; you're among your own kind."

The d'Alemberts allowed the guards to find their two ministunners, although the search was less strenuous than they expected. Jules thought of all the miniaturized electronic gadgetry he could have smuggled under the noses of these security people, but then realized that there would have been little point to it. All the micro-equipment in the Galaxy would not get them off the planet again. They would need a spaceship for that—and the guards controlled the access to the spaceport quite thoroughly.

The SOTE agents weren't worried about being disarmed. The guards, who seemed to be plentiful, were quite well armed with both blasters and stunners. The two DesPlainians felt perfectly capable of tapping that resource when the time came. "The best agent," their father had told them many times, "is the one who's capable of improvising. If you plan things out too thoroughly beforehand, something's bound to go wrong somewhere along the line and leave you stranded."

After the search, they waited in the line to receive temporary quarters, much the same way that Helena did upon her arrival. Their interview went without a hitch, and they did nothing to arouse the suspicions of the clerk, so their pictures were not flashed directly to Garst—which was a lucky thing. Had he seen them, he would have ordered them killed on the spot. He remembered only too well how this pair of agents demolished his organization back on Vesa.

But Jules and Yvette looked to be exactly what they claimed, so the photo images of them were attached to their records and routinely filed away. Such was the advantage of a solid cover identity.

Like all new arrivals, the d'Alemberts were assigned

to temporary quarters until they decided where they wanted to live. Their rooms were in a wooden barracks building and, while more spacious than the cabins aboard ship, were still a far cry from the luxuries they had been led to expect. The literature they were given, however, explained that they could take their pick of any style accommodations they could afford, from economical to extravagant.

"Wow, look at some of these places," Yvette exclaimed to her brother. Both agents were sure that these rooms, too, were bugged, so they were being very careful to watch what they said while indoors. "I want to live in an apartment like this," and she pointed to one set of pictures that, true to real-estate-brochure form, were more beautiful than true.

Jules looked at the picture his sister indicated, and pretended to be concerned about their financial state. "We can't afford that," he said flatly. "We'll take a two-bedroom place like this one over here instead. At a hundred and fifty rubles a month, it'll allow us a little more spending money for other things we may need."

They had a mock argument on the subject, with Yvette eventually giving in. "You're always too practical," she declared.

The next day they moved into a two-bedroom apartment similar to the one in the brochure, though not as picture perfect. Yvette admitted grudgingly that it would be acceptable, and the argument ended there.

In the meantime, too, they had been reading the bookreel they'd been given entitled YOUR GUIDE TO SANCTUARY. At present the planet contained only the one city, which had a population of over 27,000. Of that population, almost two-thirds were "refugees" like the d'Alemberts, with the rest being employees of the government—service personnel to perform the tasks that needed doing. The clients could take it easy in what was essentially a retirement village.

No effort had been spared in an attempt to keep the immigrants happy with their new lives. The community was beautifully planned, with apartment buildings skillfully blended into the natural landscape. Nothing was crowded together. There were parks and greenery everywhere one looked, and the effect was most pleasing to the eye. There were plenty of swimming pools and gymnasia, sports areas, shops, theaters, restaurants, bars, casinos and other places where the newly located citizens could pass their time without fear of the police.

A more critical observer would have noticed some important omissions in the book's text, however. Nowhere was there any mention of government, or how the people might regulate their own lives. There was no mention of communicating with anyone offworld. And nowhere did it say a word about leaving the planet again. Ever.

Sanctuary was, in reality, a penitentiary without bars. Luxury plus, it was true, but a prison nonetheless. The inmates must have realized that fact, at least on a subconscious level. For the most part these were people who had lived hard lives as criminals, and they could not easily adjust to unlimited leisure. Drinks and drugs were consumed on a vast scale, and scarcely a day went by without several major brawls erupting in the bars.

Sanctuary, at best, was an imperfect paradise.

Now that the d'Alemberts were finally here, they could concentrate on their real assignment, which was to find Helena and make sure she'd be able to escape from here safely. Jules had thought this would mean his sister would finally stop seeing Nav socially and work with him again. To his chagrin, he found this was not so.

"Look at it this way," Yvette said as the two of them

were taking a stroll along an isolated path. They had found themselves taking a lot of walks since coming here; it was one way of making sure their conversations would not be bugged. "There are more than 27,000 people here, and we're looking for one particular one. We'll double our chances of spotting her if we split up and look individually. If Pias wants to escort me all over the city, what better excuse for me to be out and looking at things? That'll leave you free to look in the places where I don't go."

The fact that her plan was contradictory to his own wishes and yet made so much sense at the same time only served to make Jules more upset. "He's not being honest with you," he insisted. "There's something more sinister in him than he's showing."

"You keep making these vague accusations. You've been keeping a close watch on him for over a week now; haven't you learned anything more definite?"

Reluctantly, then, Jules told her about Nav's strange behavior in Carnery's cabin the second day aboard ship. Yvette listened attentively, then was silent for a long moment after her brother had finished. "I knew there was something unusual between Pias and Carnery; I could feel it from the very first moment Pias spoke about the man. *Khorosho,* so maybe he has a personal grudge against Carnery for some reason. Is that any excuse for me not to like him?"

"You didn't see the expression on his face. I tell you, that man is dangerous."

"All men are dangerous," Yvette smiled. "That's one of the first lessons a girl learns when she grows up. If we let that stop us, the human race would have been extinct millennia ago. Is that all the evidence you have against him?"

"No. He's lying to us about his identity, too. I found

89

a handkerchief in his cabin with the monogram 'PB' in one corner."

"We're lying to him about our identities, too, you know. I'm not really Yarmilla Dubcek. I can see a number of circumstances where it might be convenient for a professional gambler to change his name frequently. It's not the name I care about, it's the person behind it. He's a good man, Julie; I know that as surely as I know anything in the Universe."

She leaned over and kissed her brother lightly on the forehead. "It's very sweet of you to be so concerned about me, really it is. I know it's because you love me, and I love you too. But remember, I'm a year older than you are. I can take care of myself, honestly I can. We're not Siamese twins, I do have a life of my own. I don't begrudge you the time you spend with Vonnie, please grant me the same courtesy."

She glanced at her ringwatch. "I really don't have time to talk about it further right now—I promised to meet Pias in ten more minutes, and if I hurry I can just make it. I'll keep in mind what you've told me about him, and I'll keep my eyes open for any sign of Helena at the same time. That is my primary purpose here, and I know that as well as you do. But let me do it in my own way. *A bientôt.*" And she walked hurriedly away, leaving Jules to feel very frustrated by his inability to convinct her of Nav's dangerous potential.

She's making an idiot of herself, he thought angrily. But he realized at the same time that his sister was a very strong-willed woman, and that he was not going to change her mind with a couple of words. Putting her problem out of his mind for the moment, he concentrated on looking for Helena instead.

Yvette met Pias Nav at a restaurant that specialized in Nagalese food. Although he was already seated at a table right in front, she pretended not to spot him immediately, which gave her the opportunity to give the room a general scan. There was no sign of Helena, so she acknowledged Nav's wave and went to sit beside him.

He stood up as she approached and bent to kiss her hand, as was his custom. They ordered the specialty of the house, which was a platter of raw fish with a large side helping of vegetables dipped in batter and deep fat fried. There was a wide variety of sauces in which to dip their foods, which made the meal an exploration into a broad range of taste treats.

Midway through the meal, the Newforester suddenly looked up at her and changed the topic of their hitherto innocuous conversation. "Your brother doesn't like me, does he?"

"What do you mean?"

"I'm not blind, Yarmilla. Whenever he's in the same room with us I can feel those icy stares he sends me. And the curtness of his words is indication enough that he really doesn't want to talk to me much. Is he giving you a hard time because of me?"

"He *is* upset," Yvette said slowly. As she spoke she was wondering how to phrase herself in the most diplomatic way possible. "He feels very protective, even though I'm a bit older than he is. Our family pride is very strong, and he's afraid I might marry beneath our station."

Pias Nav gave a brief chuckle.

"What's so funny?" Yvette asked him.

With an effort, the Newforester returned his face to its previous serious countenance. "Oh, nothing really. I, uh, was just wondering how far below your station I was. I'm a gambler and you're a cat burglar, after all. We both rate pretty low on the scale."

Yvette cursed herself for the slip. Their father was

the Duke of the planet DesPlaines, though he preferred to travel with the Circus as its Manager. Marriages between nobility and commoners were routine, and even encouraged in some circles, so there could be no legal bar to Yvette's marrying Nav if she chose; nevertheless, she was certain their rank was one factor weighing on Jules's mind. But stating it the way she had did give the impression that her origins were loftier than she was admitting.

Fortunately, the Newforester seemed to be treating her statement almost as a joke. In this context, it was ludicrous to be worried about her "station."

"I don't think Jaro would consider *any* man good enough for me," Yvette elucidated. "Fraternal jealousy is a very strong motivational force. But perhaps you wouldn't know about that."

"Indeed I would," Nav replied. "I have three sisters myself. Two of them married men whom I consider total louts; the third is only sixteen, so I haven't had the chance to worry much about her yet. But I know the worry a brother goes through. Especially on Newforest—we consider our women almost sacred there. The ancient customs die hard."

He looked at Yvette for a long, silent minute and then repeated, "Very sacred."

Yvette's mouth was suddenly dry, but she forced herself to keep her tone light as she asked the next important question. "Does my brother's opinion really matter that much to you?"

"Yes." Nav barely whispered the word, but it hung in the air between them as though he'd shouted it. "That is, it should, except . . . I don't know anymore, I really don't. I shouldn't let it affect me so. We're just a couple of wayfarers who have happened to this place together; we should enjoy ourselves and not think much about the future, correct?"

Yvette had never seen her friend so serious. The confusion of his thoughts seemed almost a mirror to her own. "Yes, that's very much the way I felt. Things work out so strangely at times; we may have to part and never see one another again, so why should we get more strongly involved than we are now?"

"Exactly," he nodded. "Marriage and the like is completely out of the question."

"I never brought the subject up."

"And I never meant to," he said slowly. "Let's forget I did." He stared down at his nearly empty plate. "I think I've had about all the food I want, right now. Let's go for a walk, shall we?"

Once outside in the open air, his mood brightened considerably. The location of this city had been chosen primarily for its mild climate, and the weather today was even more perfect than normal. The sunshine quickly restored the gaiety to his voice. They walked hand in hand across the cool grass of a nearby park, not saying much when suddenly, on impulse, he turned to her and said, "I know what let's do. Let's go to a sensable show."

"Great idea," she smiled back.

He had his hat—with its ever-present fresh red rose—in his hand, and waved it about excitedly. "A very romantic one—melodrama with a happy ending, hero and heroine deeply in love despite all obstacles and a kiss at the fadeout."

Yvette laughed as Pias mimed a swordfight, stabbing his imaginary adversary at last with a comical flourish. "Yes, *touché*," she said. "That's exactly what we need. Lead on, milord, lead on!"

The two young people walked to a streetcorner and pushed a button on the call post. Within two minutes, an automated two-seater cart buzzed quietly to a stop in front of them and they got in. Nav dialed the code for the public sensable theater, and the screen in front lit up to tell him how much it would cost to drive there from here. Nav obediently dropped seven twenty-kopek pieces into the slot and began the leisurely drive to their destination.

The cart proceeded along at its standard pace of fifteen kilometers an hour. On the street, they passed several other similar carts, traveling at more or less the same speed. These carts were the only public methods of transportation on the planet, though the d'Alemberts surmised that the guards had vehicles that could travel much faster if they needed to get somewhere in a real hurry. The lack of speedy transportation added to the leisurely atmosphere of Sanctuary—and, incidentally, would serve to keep any rebellion on the part of the inmates from getting out of hand. Jules and Yvette had been properly impressed by the ingenuity of the system.

Nav and Yvette arrived at the theater and found a private booth of their own. The two of them looked down the list of available shows and discussed their choice at length, finally settling on a costume epic set in Renaissance France. Then, leaning back in the special chairs, they prepared to enjoy the show.

In principle, the sensable projector worked much the same way a stun-gun did. Each device shot a special beam at its target that affected the nervous system of the recipient. In the case of a stunner, the effects would be paralysis, unconsciousness or even death, depending on the setting used. The projector, however, had effects that were much more intricate than that.

The sensable, in brief, took over all the senses of the body and played its show to them, rather than just the senses of sight and sound as previous media had done. The person undergoing the experience was not merely a viewer, he was a participant in the action itself. Although his mind remained aware that he was physically seated within a sensable booth, all his senses told him that he was experiencing the story that was happening around him. He could see and hear the events as his "character" felt them; he was assailed by the scents of the scene; if the "character" ate, he could taste the foods. Anything the "character" felt—pain, pleasure, running, standing—the participant also experienced. In essence, the participant was a puppet, acting out the story the play's creators told while still sitting comfortably in a chair in the sensable booth. It was perhaps the ultimate in vicarious entertainment.

The show that Nav and Yvette were experiencing was one designed specifically for a romantic couple. There were two major roles, the hero and heroine, and the two participants acted out their parts with great relish. Yvette particularly found her role diverting. The heroine was a passive woman who needed the hero to rescue her from all sorts of dire circumstances. In real life she would never have put up with such a state of affairs, but she thought it was amusing in a fictional context.

They left the theater in a very exhilarated state, completely recovered from the upset their dinner conversation had brought about. "I've always felt that I belonged in an era like that one," Nav remarked as he punched the button on the call post for another cart. "Look at the situation of the Universe today. Where are the great Romantics who would languish for a rose? Who scaled milady's balcony and swung upon her drape? They've flown like ashes, I'm afraid, leaving the world to shopkeepers and accountants."

"There's always you," Yvette said admiringly.

"Yes, we reappear in flashes, relics of a long-lamented age—but we find ourselves contrary to the vogue," he sighed. "I feel perpetually as though I should go around with a sword and a rose and a cape."

"The rose and the cape you've got. The sword would be illegal in many places and wouldn't go at all with your wardrobe."

"As well as meeting with such astonished eyebrows," Nav agreed. Their cart arrived and the Newforester helped Yvette climb inside before getting in himself. "Where to?" he asked.

"My home," Yvette replied. "I'm afraid I'm feeling very tired. I've been living too long on lighter gravity worlds; I'm starting to fatigue a bit more easily than I should."

"The same with me. What I wouldn't give to be back on Newforest right now, sitting in a glade in the woods with some *real* gravity pulling on me, whistling a gypsy tune."

Nav inserted the indicated fare and drove the cart in the direction of Yvette's apartment. Neither of them spoke much as they rode. Yvette cuddled up against the Newforester's strong masculine body and basked in the warmth of their relationship. He felt so right for her; their personalities, their desires, their thoughts matched one another so well. And yet she knew, down deep within herself, that what her brother was trying to tell her was true. She would finish her assignment here, hopefully in the near future, and then move on to some other hazardous job. Pias—well, he would probably move on, too, to follow his own particular destiny.

Yvette gave a small sigh. All the ifs were so lovely that it seemed a shame to tarnish them with reality.

They came to the corner of the street where Yvette's apartment building was, and there the cart stopped. The two of them got out and walked with their arms around each other's waist down the narrow pathway fifty meters to Yvette's door. Their good-night kiss lasted five minutes, and even then they were reluctant to pull away from each other. Yvette was seriously tempted to invite him inside, no matter what Jules would think of it; but then she remembered the dinnertime conversation and decided that, if she were to survive this affair at all, she would have to keep it on a surface level. Finally she just said, "I have to go in, now."

Her escort nodded. "I'll be in touch with you in the next day or so. After all, we'll be here for a long time; we'll probably end up becoming bored with ourselves."

Yvette nodded and kissed the tip of his nose as she sent him on his way. She stood with the door open until he made it to the corner. She could hear the Gypsy whistling as he walked casually down the path to the street.

The next morning as the two SOTE agents went for a walk, Jules asked her how she had fared the night before. "No sign of Helena," she answered, evading the real meaning of his question.

"I haven't found her yet, either. It's becoming very frustrating. What if they've already spotted her and killed her? We could look for years and never see anything."

"Let's not give up hope just yet. There's 27,000 people living here; we can't expect to see everyone in the first couple of days."

"It would certainly help, though, if you would stop seeing so much of one particular person."

Yvette exploded. "Listen. Brother or not, you have no right to intrude in my affairs this way. I'm getting tired of your constant carping. Pias has been nothing but charming and polite to me since the first moment we met. And even if he were to turn suddenly into the Beast of the Upper Galaxy, I'm perfectly capable of defending myself, thank you."

Jules struggled to maintain his own temper. "I just can't help remembering," he said slowly, "that Paul Symond was incredibly handsome and charming, too—and that we learned one of Rustin's robots was built in the shape of a male from a high-grav planet."

The argument took Yvette by surprise. She stopped walking and gave a tiny gasp. Paul Symond had been the first of the robots they discovered, built specifically to be attractive to women—and to one woman in particular: Crown Princess Edna. Dr. Rustin and his superior, Duke Fyodor of Kolokov, had been intending to have their creation marry the Princess and thus gain some control over the affairs of Empire. The actions of the d'Alembert family had broken up that plot; but, as they well knew, there were still some robots unaccounted for. And Yvette herself had been there when they discovered the fact that there was a high-grav male on the list.

When she regained her tongue, she sputtered, "That's impossible, he couldn't be . . ."

"How can you be so sure? Symond was an awfully good imposter. It took special detection equipment for us to spot him positively, and we don't have any of it with us now."

Yvette sat down on a nearby rock and stared blankly out into space. "He's real, I know he is."

"You could stick a pin in him to see if he bleeds."

"You can be a cruel man, *frère* Jules." A trace of banter was starting to return to her voice, but Jules could detect the turmoil and indecision lying beneath the surface.

Suddenly his anger at her deserted him. She was his sister, after all, and he shouldn't be trying to hurt her. "I'm not saying he is a robot," Jules soothed. "I'm just saying that people in our position can't be too careful. He probably isn't, as a matter of fact; that would be one hell of a coincidence, wouldn't it? But we're in the middle of enemy territory right now, all alone, and we may be fighting for our lives at any moment. We have to be positive about every step we take, *n'est-ce pas?*"

"*Oui.*" She looked up into his face. Was it his imagination, or did he see the glimmer of a tear in her eye? Whatever it was he thought he saw, it was gone in a second. "All I know," she said in an even tone, "is that I can't help feeling what I do for him, any more than you can help feeling what you do for Vonnie. I promise, though, that I'll be a good little agent and not let my feelings interfere with the performance of my duties."

"I never doubted *that* for a second." Jules gave her an encouraging smile, his first in almost a week. "I think we should split up for the rest of the day. Why don't you take this side of town and I'll roam around the west side, and see what we can pick up."

"All smooth," she agreed, fully in control of herself once more. Jules left her, then, without a qualm and took one of the public carts to a shopping center on the west side of town, where he proceeded to browse around the mall, looking more at the people than at the merchandise.

After two hours without success, he was just about to give up and try a new location when he saw her. Helena was coming out of a store with a small package under her arm, and she began walking off in the direction opposite to him.

Jules's heart gave an extra beat. Helena was still alive! That at least quashed the worst of the fears he and his sister had entertained. That left them with two major questions. The first was, how much had she learned about this operation . . . and the second, much more important, was, how were the three of them going to get off this planet alive?

CHAPTER 8

Razzle Dazzle

Jules was about to go after her when his sharp eyes noticed one other detail: Helena was being followed. A man who had been lounging against a wall across the way suddenly straightened up and began walking parallel to her path. The man's demeanor was casual, and he expressed no overt interest in Helena's destination, but Jules was not fooled. He'd had sufficient training—and he'd done enough tail work himself—to know when something looked suspicious. Looking through the crowd, he spotted another tail on Helena as well—this time a woman. That, he supposed, was so that Helena would not be able to use the time-honored trick of dodging into the ladies' 'freshers and leaving the male shadow waiting outside while she disappeared out the window.

Jules's heart sank. If the people behind this conspiracy were worried enough about her to put *two* tails on her, Helena's cover must be completely broken. And yet they were still letting her roam free. To Jules, that could mean only one thing—that they were confident enough of their security to know they could take her in at any time. She obviously, then, was being used as bait to trap any other SOTE agents in the neighborhood—like himself and Yvette. The d'Alemberts dared not approach her until they had made sufficient arrangements to protect their own covers.

At the same time, now that he'd finally spotted her he couldn't let her get away until he knew where she could be reached; he couldn't count on finding her accidentally again. Making sure to appear casual himself—and ascertaining that there was no one following him—he set off after Helena and her two tails.

The surreptitious parade wandered through the shopping area, with Helena stopping at two more stores for small items. Then she pressed a button on the corner call post and waited for a cart to come by. Jules went to a different corner and summoned a cart of his own. The two shadows, he noted, did the same thing. The carts were passenger driven; as long as he kept dropping coins in, there was no limit to how far he could go. Consequently, he didn't worry about his quarry getting away. At fifteen kilometers an hour, she couldn't go too far too fast.

Hc followed her to an apartment, where she entered and closed the door. Her two other followers took up what looked to be, to them, familiar positions from which they could watch the doorway. This, then, must be Helena's apartment and, like Jules's own, it undoubtedly had only the one door. Jules made a note of the address and drove on by, making sure he was not noticed by the two followers.

One hurdle had been overcome: he knew now that Helena was alive and where she was located. The next problem was a tricky matter of logistics—how could he communicate with her without revealing his identity to the people who were tailing her? He certainly couldn't walk up to her door; the tails would be instructed to make note of anyone contacting her. Helena's com line was bound to be tapped; even if he called her from a public booth and spoke entirely in code, the people tapping her would be aware that she was in contact with someone else and would be alerted. He could wait until she went out on another errand, then break into her apartment and leave a note—except that her apartment was likely to be bugged with both microphones and cameras, and he would be spotted, photographed and identified.

Jules parked his cart and walked along the street, considering the problem. Finally the solution occurred to him. He walked to a nearby stationery store and bought a notepad, a pen and a box of chalk. Then he went to a bench in a park and carefully composed a note in SOTE's highest level code. Deciphered, the note began: "Call the following number at exactly seven P.M.: 84–76–873. It's a public phone at the Beechwood Cafe. One of us will answer. Say you dialed a wrong number and hang up immediately." The note went on to give further instructions for arranging a private meeting between them.

With the message completed, he looked around until he found a rock of adequate size and took it with him back to the corner nearest Helena's apartment. He put the rock down next to the corner call post, with the piece of paper under it, one edge barely visible. At this position he was out of sight of Helena's two followers at the door and, when he was sure that no one else was watching, he took a piece of chalk and scrawled a bit of graffiti on the call post. It was a heart; in the upper corner he wrote the name "Wombat" (his own code designation) and in the lower side diagonally opposite he wrote "Periwinkle" (Yvette's code name). Through the middle of the heart he drew an arrow.

To the casual eye, the scrawling would look like just the work of some immature mind, the sort of thing that was seen on all planets all over the Galaxy. Nobody would stop to think that there weren't any children on Sanctuary, and they would ignore the writing. It was something that civilized people learned to tune out of their minds.

But Helena's was not a casual eye. Jules knew from previous experience just how quickly she was able to grasp seemingly innocent signals and decipher them immediately. That call post was the one closest to Helena's apartment, and was the one she would almost certainly use when summoning a cart. The two code names would register instantly in her file-like mind. Her eye would follow in the direction of the arrow, which pointed directly at the rock. She would find some excuse to bend down casually and examine it, notice the paper and palm it, to read in private.

Jules gave his handiwork one quick skim to make sure it was perfect, then walked quickly away. The longer he dawdled here, the more chance he had of arousing suspicion. The plan had been put in motion; the next step would be up to Helena.

He walked two blocks to the next closest call post and was about to summon a cart to take him home when he spotted Pias Nav across the street. The gambler was just emerging from an alleyway, looking both ways as though to be sure no one was observing him. He didn't see Jules standing across the street more than sixty meters away. He wiped his hands nervously on the sides of his jumpsuit and walked briskly in the opposite direction.

Jules stopped and wondered at this strange behavior. *Something happened in that alley that he doesn't want to be associated with,* he thought. *And whatever it is, I want to know about it—for Evie's sake.*

Crossing the street, he walked with feigned casualness to the mouth of the alleyway. The space between the two buildings was narrow and the buildings were high, shutting out most of the light and making it hard to see. Cautiously, Jules picked his way over and around scattered boxes and trash that littered the ground, until he came to a dead end. He looked around, but saw nothing unusual at first glance. He was about to start out toward the street again, disappointed, when he nearly slipped on a wet spot of ground. Leaning down closer, he saw that it was a small pool of fresh blood.

The pool was fed by a little stream that emanated from a large overturned box one meter away. Jules went over to it and lifted the carton to see what was under it.

There lay the body of Rowe Carnery. The pirate had been tied up very securely and gagged so that he could not make a sound. Then both his wrists and throat had been slashed, quite neatly. His clothing was soaked in his own blood, and his eyes stared openly in glassy horror. He had been dead for a little while, at least.

Even Jules's steady nerves were a little shaken by the sight. He set the box down again and took a step backward, leaning against the wall so that he could think.

As far as he was concerned, this clinched his case against Pias Nav. Yvette would not be able to excuse away such a barbaric, deliberate murder as this. The man was a ruthless killer, not to be trusted.

Rowe Carnery was not his concern. Virtually everyone on this planet was here because he had committed enough crimes to fill several books. Jules didn't care if they all murdered one another—it would save himself and the imperial courts a lot of trouble. But his sister *was* his concern. She would have to be told about this before she became any more deeply involved with the gambler from Newforest.

It was not a task he was looking forward to.

As he'd feared, she took it pretty hard.

He had gone back to their apartment and waited for her to return. A brief hand signal indicated there was something he wanted to talk to her about privately, so they went out on one of their habitual walks. He told her first about finding Helena and leaving the message, which thrilled her completely. While she was still on the peak of excitement, thinking about what their plans should be from this point, he told her what he had seen after planting the message.

Yvette was stunned. She sat down on a large nearby rock and stared blankly out into empty air. "I can't believe it," she muttered, half to herself.

"I wouldn't lie about a thing like that."

She shook her head. "I know that. It's just . . . I *know* Pias. Or at least I thought I knew him. I would never have believed him capable of anything like that. He had a few faults, but on the whole he seemed to prefer to avoid trouble. You don't think there's any chance that someone else committed the murder and he just stumbled across Carnery's body by accident, do you?"

Jules cleared his throat. "Well, I suppose it *is* possible. But in the back of a dark, narrow alley, where he had no business being in the first place? And after the look I saw on his face in Carnery's cabin aboard ship? Maybe one chance in a billion, but those aren't odds I'd care to bet."

Yvette closed her eyes and bowed her head down. Jules could tell that she was fighting back a stream of tears. "*Tu as raison,* as always. I knew it, but I had to ask the question." She shook her head slowly from side to side. "I knew from that first meal aboard ship that something was not right between Pias and Carnery. Pias's tone was slightly off when he spoke about Carnery. Yet it seemed to be a one-sided thing; Carnery took no notice of him."

She pounded her fist repeatedly against the rock on which she sat. "Oh Pias, why, why, why? Why did you have to do it? Why did it all have to be here and now? Why did things have to be the way they are?"

Jules stood beside her and put a hand on her shoulder. "I'm afraid I can't give you any explanation."

"I was thirty years old last month, and still without any 'prospects,' as they say. You must admit, for our family that's pretty unusual. Most of our women are married and tending large families by this time."

"Well, even in our family, you're pretty unusual. Any woman can have a husband and kids; how many of them can save the Empire as often as you have?"

Yvette looked up, a watery smile on her face. She patted her brother's hand. "You have the habit, *mon frère,* of injecting business matters into the most intimate of conversations. Yes, of course you're right, I do have a higher obligation. There are already plenty of our relatives busily engaged in prolonging the family line. We have work to do."

Her eyes were dry by now, her voice level. Her body was still trembling slightly, but it was coming more under control. She was back to being Yvette d'Alembert, secret agent extraordinaire for the Service of the Empire—a top professional doing what she did best. Pias Nav was, if not totally forgotten, at least relegated to a distant corner of her mind where he could be locked away until there was the time available to go into that matter at leisure.

"The way I see it, then," she went on, "we hang around the Beechwood Cafe at seven P.M. tonight; if she doesn't call, we assume she didn't spot the message yet, and go back there tomorrow."

"*Au juste.* If she misses three nights in a row, we check up on her and try something else. I don't think she will, though—she's a clever girl."

"Not too clever. She's got two people tailing her every move, and probably more electronic gadgetry in her

106

house than a mad inventor."

"It could be she knows she's being watched and just has not had the need to shake her tails off yet."

Yvette shook her head. "Call it a hunch, but that's not the way I read the situation. Remember, Helena's had all the training but not a lick of practical experience. She got involved in this business because she wanted to show us all that she could handle the job. I'm willing to bet she's so wrapped up in her own infallibility she hasn't even considered the possibility that she's been spotted. You said those tails were pretty good and, subconsciously, Helena doesn't *want* to see them there."

"She'll know they're there when she gets my note; I told her so quite explicitly."

"Poor girl, it'll probably be something of a blow to her ego. But she'll survive it, I think. I only wish we knew some way of getting off this planet again. We've been so busy looking for her that we haven't really had a chance to explore that situation."

"She may be able to help us there. She's been here for weeks, observing conditions. She must know something about the schedule of incoming and outgoing ships, how things are organized and guarded, and so on. With her knowledge and our diabolical cunning, we should be able to manage something."

"Overweening modesty certainly isn't one of your shortcomings, is it? *Alors,* we dine tonight at the Beechwood Cafe and hope to receive a com call at seven from a 'wrong number.' "

They were at the restaurant at six-thirty and ordered their meal. They specifically requested a booth towards the back, near the public com unit. At five minutes before seven, Yvette got up from the table and stationed herself beside the instrument. She tried to remain casual and not look at her ringwatch as the minutes crept past toward the appointed hour.

At precisely seven o'clock, the unit began buzzing. Yvette let it buzz for several seconds, then—when she could stand the suspense no longer—she picked up the receiver, making sure the visual transmit button was off, and said, "Hello?"

"Oh, I'm terribly sorry," came Helena's welcome voice. "I must have dialed the wrong number." And, as instructed, she clicked off immediately.

Yvette went back to the table and reported to her brother. "Connections completed."

Jules gave a tiny nod. "We'd better finish our dinner then and get home to sleep. We've got an important meeting tomorrow."

The operation designed to shake off Helena's tails was scheduled to begin at noon the next day in the same shopping center where Jules had first spotted Helena. The Head's Girl Friday appeared promptly when she was supposed to and began walking into a certain restaurant, as though to have lunch before doing her shopping. The two shadows started to follow her inside, but their plans were interrupted by two timely "accidents."

Yvette d'Alembert, carrying an awkward armload of packages, collided with the female follower, scattering boxes in all directions. "Now look what you've done, you clumsy oaf," Yvette shrieked. "I sure as hell hope nothing got broken in there. Did you hear anything break?"

"No," said the other woman, anxious to be away from this scene and back to following her target. "No, I don't think so. I'm in kind of a hurry . . ."

"Sure, I'll bet you are," Yvette said shrilly. She grabbed the woman's arm as the other tried to slip away from her. "That's what gives you the right to knock people down and scatter their packages from one end of the block to the other, isn't it? If you wouldn't be in so much of a hurry, maybe you could take the time to look where you're going. Maybe you wouldn't be running into total strangers like this."

Yvette's whining voice was beginning to draw a crowd, which was the last thing the other woman wanted. It is not good form for a shadow to draw attention. This whole business was becoming very embarrassing. "Listen, I'm very sorry, truly I am, but . . ."

"What good does 'sorry' do me, huh? Does it help me pick up my packages that are all over the sidewalk?" Yvette started limping exaggeratedly on one leg, while still holding onto the other woman's arm. "And on top of everything else, I think I sprained my ankle when you knocked me down."

"I didn't knock you down . . ."

"Then why are my packages all over the street? Do you think I just threw them there for my health? Why is my ankle throbbing with pain? It feels like it's going to fall off any second. It's all your fault."

"Look, I said I'm sorry, now let me go!" The woman pushed Yvette away and started off in the direction Helena had taken. Yvette could have tried to stall her some more, but it would have been too much. She didn't want to divert any more suspicion onto herself than was necessary. She had held up the tail long enough for Helena to do what was required; it was now up to the Girl Friday to see if she did indeed have what it took to be a secret agent.

The male follower, meanwhile—oblivious to the fate of his comrade—had actually gotten into the restaurant after Helena. Here, however, Jules was ready with a similar ploy. As the man walked quickly to keep up with Helena's increasing pace, Jules stepped in front of him with a tray full of food and cold drinks. The contents ended up being spilled all down the front of the shadow's clothing.

"Oh, I'm dreadfully sorry, I didn't see you," Jules said in an apologetic manner that would have won him the Galaxy Award for acting "Here, let me help you wipe some of that mess off."

"That really isn't necessary," the other man said hastily. His only thought was getting out of here quickly and after Helena.

"No, really, I insist." Jules took the man's wrist in an unbreakable grip and led him over to one table where there was a pile of napkins. His mien was so self-deprecating that the other man was not really aware that he had no choice in the matter. Jules was strong enough to drag a horse if he chose.

"Please, I have to meet someone," the man protested.

"This will only take a second, relax," Jules assured the fellow in soothing tones. "And besides, we don't want to stain that nice outfit you're wearing, do we?" With exaggerated neatness he wiped and dabbed at the spots on the front of the other man's suit with his right hand while holding the man firmly in place with the left. He reached over and dipped the corner of one napkin in a glass of cold water that was standing nearby. "This will keep some of those spots from setting in permanently," he blathered on. "It's a trick my mother taught me."

"I don't give a dancing drap for your mother," the follower said furiously. He tried to tug gently away from Jules's grip and found that was impossible, so he gave a mighty heave with all his strength. Jules chose that instant to let go, with the result that the man tumbled heels over head backwards over the table, crashing into another pair of diners and spilling *their* food all over the floor.

Stunned, the man tried to pick himself up off the

110

ground and Jules, ever helpful, went over to lend him assistance. The man had almost reached a standing position when Jules's foot "slipped." Actually, Jules used a smooth bit of judo to flip the man over, but the results were the same: the hapless shadow landed hard on the floor once more. This time he was even more stunned, and did not try to get up immediately.

"Don't help me!" he snarled as Jules approached him again. "I'm perfectly capable of handling this on my own, thank you."

"You haven't done too well so far," Jules commented quietly.

The man got slowly to his feet, muttering some very uncomplimentary things about Jules under his breath. At that moment the man's partner burst through the door. She looked around and saw her comrade in sorry disarray, with no sign of Helena. She knew the girl she was following had not gone out the front door, so she hurried around to the back, with her coworker hot on her heels.

The restaurant did have a back door, which led out onto an alley. Several other shops had back doors which also led out into the same alley, but there was no one in sight. The woman pointed for her friend to go to the right while she moved left. They each went to their respective ends, but there was no trace of Helena on either side. Trying the doors as they came back down the alley, they found them all locked from the inside.

By the time they returned to the inside of the restaurant, there was no sign of the two people whose "clumsiness" had delayed them. They had vanished as efficiently as Helena.

Fearfully, the two people went to the nearest vidicom booth to inform their boss that they had lost their target. Garst would not be pleased.

As soon as she saw Jules begin his act, Helena moved into action. Jules had told her in his note that he would have a cart waiting in the alley out back of the restaurant, and indeed there was one. He had fed it with plenty of coins and left its motor running so that it wouldn't be recalled to the local dispatching station. Now Helena hopped in quickly and drove off down the alley to the street. Its fifteen-kilometer-an-hour pace was infuriatingly slow in this situation, and Helena felt she could make better time on foot. She could have, at least as far as the end of the alley, but Jules had been thinking of long distance movement. Running would move her faster, but would wear her out and her pursuers might be able to catch up with her. The carts were slower but steadier, and could go indefinitely.

Helena drove her cart around the corner and merged with the general traffic. It being lunchtime, there were a good many other carts on the street as well, and it was easy for her to lose herself in the flow. After driving for twenty minutes in a most circuitous route, she came to the park Jules had designated as the rendezvous spot. She left the cart then and walked to the specific stand of trees Jules had mentioned in his note.

The d'Alemberts joined her within three minutes. Their descriptions were not as well known—the followers had seen them only for a couple of minutes, under harried circumstances—and so they did not need to take as much precaution getting here.

"Oh, it's so good to see the two of you again," Helena said, kissing Jules and Yvette in turn. "But what are you both doing here?"

"Looking after you," Jules said sternly. "A person with your responsibilities simply has no right to go gallivanting off into danger anytime she has a mind to. If the knowledge you're carrying in your head should

112

reach the wrong people, all of SOTE would be in trouble."

"But . . ." Helena started to protest.

"Plus," Yvette added, cutting her off, "your father is worried to death about you. If you refuse to deal on a professional level, think on a personal level. Is it right for you to treat him this way?"

"You could have been killed at any time," Jules went on with the harangue. "You still could, even more now that you've slipped your tail. Is it worth it?"

Helena hung her head. "I'm sorry."

"Yes, and I'll bet you'll be sorrier by the time we get you home. *If* we get you home," Yvette added ominously. "But right now, we're more concerned about *getting* you there; the spanking can come later. You've been here several weeks now at least. What have you learned about the place that might help us?"

"Not nearly as much as I would have liked," Helena admitted. "I've learned virtually nothing about whoever's running the show. The administration is performed very quietly and secretively here; they don't want much publicity. I *have* learned that things seem to be controlled from a complex over on the north side of town, less than a kilometer from the spaceport. There's a series of low, white buildings with no particularly solid looking defenses in front. But the guards seem to spend an awful lot of time in that section. The address is 666 Crowley Drive. I'm convinced something is going on inside there, but I haven't been able to get in yet to check up on it."

"No visible defenses may mean they've got some pretty sophisticated stuff," Jules mused. "Or it may mean there's nothing there worth guarding. It's hard to tell at this point. What about ships? We'll need some method of transportation if we're going to get away from here."

"There's always plenty of ships on the spaceport field. Sanctuary has no agriculture and no industry. It imports *everything*. That's why the prices are so scandalous."

Yvette gave a low whistle. "And they support 27,000 people here, day in and day out. That must take an enormous organization."

"It would take a hundred ships a day to bring in all the food," Jules mused aloud.

"Yes, and that only scratches the surface. The luxury goods have to come from somewhere, too," Helena pointed out. "I've done a good deal of figuring on this myself—I *can* think, on occasion. All these shiploads of cargo have to be coordinated. They have to be diverted from elsewhere, since this planet is not officially on anyone's charts. The paperwork alone must be staggering, the way they juggle all the shipments without letting anyone suspect where they're going."

"We're talking about an Empire-wide conspiracy," Jules said. "It might even be related to the one that started the business with the robots."

"If I hadn't seen Garst fall into that recycling vat with my own eyes," Yvette said, "I would swear this had his style to it. First, to find people disappearing without a trace. Second, because the operation is organized with such terrific efficiency. Third—well, he was First Advisor to Marchioness Gindri of Vesa, an airless moon that had to import all its goods to feed a population much larger than this. If anyone would know how to establish a setup like this, it would be him."

"I'm sure he didn't have a monopoly on those talents," Jules said. "The coincidence is strange, though. Perhaps the boss of this endeavor is someone who worked with him at one time or who has read about his methods."

Jules could see that all this talk about Garst was upsetting his sister. When the two of them had been conducting their investigation on Vesa, there'd been a man with whom Yvette had found some romantic attachment; but Dak Lehman had died, as had innumerable others, as a victim of Garst's murder and robbery ring, and Yvette still held bitter feelings about the man responsible. Garst had fallen into a vat of chemicals while Yvette was chasing him through Vesa's recycling plant, and even though that could not have been a pleasant death Yvette felt cheated of her revenge.

The talk of Garst, coming on top of the upsetting news about Pias Nav, was beginning to fray Yvette's nerves, so Jules decided to change the subject now before the conversation became even stickier. "It doesn't really matter, though, *who* is behind this operation at the moment. We have to get off Sanctuary so that we can report all of this to headquarters. The Service will be able to take care of the detail work."

Yvette nodded agreement. "The most obvious move is that we dare not go back to our respective apartments. The Boss will know by now, Helena, that you gave his people the slip, which means that you had some reason to do so. He only left you free because he thought he could keep a close eye on you; now that his game has been spoiled, he'd either have you killed or picked up for questioning the second you're spotted."

"Descriptions of us will be out, too," Jules added. "Those tails didn't get too good a look at us, but anyone who appears to resemble us even vaguely will probably be snatched."

Helena shrugged. "There's nothing worth going back for in my apartment. A few notes, perhaps, but I have them memorized. I suppose the only choice we have now is to run for the spaceport and hope to sneak aboard an outgoing ship before they think to stop us."

"Exactly." Jules knew that everything that had gone

115

before this moment—the burglaries, the chases by police, the arrival at Sanctuary under false identities—hard though they may have been, would be child's play compared to this final stage of the assignment. The entire security force of this criminal's haven would be mustered to prevent them from getting away with the information they possessed. That information would spell doom for the leaders of Sanctuary.

The trio from SOTE would have to look carefully with each step they took—for each step might well be their last.

CHAPTER 9

Ambush and Ally

Garst slammed his fist down on his desktop in undiluted anger. "What do you mean, you lost her?" he bellowed.

The woman who'd been assigned to follow Helena wilted visibly. Even though she was reporting over the vidicom from the restaurant, her boss's rage was so vast that it came through full strength over the screen in front of her. "She had help," she explained weakly. "We weren't expecting it."

"That's right," added her male companion in defense. "Up until that moment, we'd had no indication she even knew we were there."

"And so you let yourselves be bummed into one of the simplest sucker games around, eh?" Garst's voice dripped cynicism. "Weren't you given special orders that she was a high SOTE official? Didn't you realize that meant she would be unusually adept? Couldn't you have figured out that one reason why we were watching her was because she might have some confederates who would help her?" He switched off the com unit in disgust, stood up, then walked once around the perimeter of his desk.

His temper only slightly cooler after this excursion, he sat down again and punched viciously at a button on his intercom. In a second, the screen lit up to show the visage of Jinda Rawling, his chief of security. "I suppose you were monitoring that last report," Garst said.

"Yes sir," the woman replied. "I have to apologize for the sheer ineptitude of my two people. I'd thought them better trained than that."

"Never mind the apologies, it's too late to do anything about that. What are you doing about picking the woman up again?"

"At your orders, sir, we placed directional beepers in all her clothes while she was out of her apartment. The beepers had to be small to avoid their being noticed, which only gives them a broadcast range of under one kilometer. I've sent teams out to sweep the city in an orderly pattern. We can cover the entire metropolitan area in an hour; with any luck, we'll relocate her in less time than that."

"Good. Keep me informed of all progress."

"Yes, sir. What do you want us to do when we find her?"

Garst weighed the various alternatives. "Maintain long distance trivision surveillance," he said after a slight pause. "Now that she thinks she's gotten away from us, she may tip her hand. I'm unhappy about that hour, though. An entire world can be lost in that time. You'd better be right, Rawling; if it takes so much as one minute more than an hour, you're out of a job."

"I'd expect nothing less, sir." Rawling was proud of her work, and even a little touchy on the subject. She had drilled her guards relentlessly, and Garst had to admit that they were one of the best-trained private forces he had ever seen.

Garst gave her a brief nod and cut the set off. He did have confidence in Rawling's abilities, even though two of her people had slipped up badly. And yet, perhaps he could work even that slip-up to his advantage. Having accomplished their ruse so easily, the SOTE forces might underestimate his defensive capabilities—which would be a lethal mistake on their part.

118

Turning to the computer outlet on his screen, he punched a set of buttons and ordered up a fax copy of the file so far on Helena von Wilmenhorst. He scanned the lines quickly, assimilating most of the information in a single glance. The young lady had been quite active in her comparatively short stay here, but had learned little of significance. She had been snooping around the headquarters complex several times, but had never been given the opportunity to get inside, so no real harm had been done there. She'd been to practically every portion of the city and probably knew her way about perfectly—but so did Rawling's guards, so there would be no advantage in that. She had spent a lot of time at the spaceport, studying the systems of arrivals and departures; well, he would see to it that her knowledge in that area was nullified, too.

On the whole, he felt he still held the upper hand. Duchess Helena knew most of the surface working of the city, but that was all. According to the reports, she had never been close to suspecting the system of underground causeways that could transport his guards to virtually any spot in the city within minutes. She was, by all indications, unarmed. Her companions were still mysteries, but even so there seemed little that they could do against his forces.

Now that SOTE had actually made its move, he was licking his lips at the excitement of the confrontation. The waiting game had been interesting, but his attention had begun to wane of late; today's action revived the struggle. It would all be coming to an end very quickly now.

There were only three alternatives open to the infiltrators as far as he could determine. One, they could leave the city, flee to the undeveloped land beyond the boundaries of Sanctuary. But they would be on foot there, without supplies for a long stay, and his troops would be

119

armed, well supplied and able to patrol the area in copters and armored cars. There would be little chance of escape that way.

Two, they could try a frontal attack on headquarters. That would net them little; they must know he would have strong defenses set up against any invasion as small as theirs. Even if they penetrated and achieved some objective inside, they would still have to get out again and off planet in order to make their achievement count—and the odds against all that happening were vanishingly small.

Three, they could try to make an escape at the spaceport. To Garst, this seemed the most likely possibility. There was a lot of traffic and frequently a lot of confusion at the port, and a casual observer might think to slip through the defenses at that point. But ever since Helena's arrival, Garst had had the guard at the spaceport quadrupled. He could send teams of reinforcements there within five minutes, should any trouble arise. To his mind, the spaceport was as secure as any place on this entire planet.

Theoretically, therefore, he should have no worries at all about the outcome of this operation. Nevertheless, he found himself staring at the face of the clock on his desk and wondering why it was taking Rawling so long to get results.

The minutes dragged slowly, and Garst found himself unable to concentrate on any of his other work. He paced around the room and reread the report on Helena twice more. Finally, forty-five minutes after Helena's disappearance, Rawling's face again appeared on the intercom screen.

"We've been able to triangulate her position, sir," the security chief reported.

"Where is she?"

"Out in a park at the moment. We'll have a long distance camera crew in a copter there in a minute so you can view the scene."

Garst waited with frantic impatience until Rawling's face was replaced by a fuzzy, wobbling image of three people in a park, sitting peacefully amid some bushes. Helena von Wilmenhorst sat in the middle, chatting as though with old friends.

But it was not Helena on whom Garst's eyes focused. The man and woman who flanked her were frighteningly familiar to him. He had met the woman once when she was calling herself Carmen Velasquez; the man, at the time, had gone under the name Georges duChamps. But he had learned, much to his sorrow, that they were two incredibly talented people who worked as a team. He knew they had worked for some law enforcement agency—and obviously, since they were friends of von Wilmenhorst, they must be agents of SOTE.

Between the two of them, they had totally demolished his organization on Vesa—an organization he had spent twenty years nurturing. It was only by a ruse that he had managed to escape with his life from the maniacal fury of that DesPlainian woman. Occasionally, in a nightmare, he would see their faces coming toward him, as though from a great distance. They would reach out their powerful hands and grab him, holding him up in the air and shaking him like a rag doll until all his stuffing flew out. He would wake from those terrifying dreams sweating and trembling; and always, the afterimage was the face of that DesPlainian woman, glaring her implacable hatred at him.

Garst found himself sweating and trembling now as he stared at the fuzzy images on the screen. He didn't know how long he had been watching, but suddenly a voice broke him out of his waking nightmare. Rawling was speaking over the picture on the viewer. "We've

121

checked their identities with our files. The names are Jaroslav and Yarmilla Dubcek, brother and sister. They came in just a couple of days ago from Cordoba."

"I don't care what they call themselves, they're poison, both of them!" Garst fairly screamed. "I've dealt with them before. They have talents that are not human. We must kill them instantly."

"Is that an order, sir?"

"Yes. They are to be shot on sight—and with blasters, not stunners. They must be given no chance to react; they're lightning incarnate."

"The copter is out of range at the moment, and if it flies any closer they might spot it coming. I could have a whole platoon of guards there in two minutes, if you like."

"Yes . . . no! They'll be making their move soon." Garst was shaking his head to clear it, trying hard to think. "There's only one reason they've come here—to get me. They've found out I'm alive and they've come to finish the job they started before. As soon as they've finished their talk they'll be on their way here to headquarters to ferret me out. But they're not going to get me, Rawling. I want you to pull every guard you've got and station them around this building. Those three are not to get in."

"All my guards? Even from the spaceport?"

"You heard me." Garst was in an unreasoning fit of terror.

"And you want all three blasted?"

"Yes. Well, if you can get the von Wilmenhorst girl alive, so much the better. But that is not first priority. Kill the other two, by any and all means possible."

In her own private office, Jinda Rawling clucked her tongue slightly. She'd never seen her boss like this, and it worried her. If something could frighten the imperturbable Garst this badly, it had to be important. She would make certain all her guards had instructions to kill those two DesPlainians on sight, no quarter given.

But, like any good tactician, she doubted the wisdom of removing *all* her people from an area as strategic as the spaceport. If Garst was right and the trio from SOTE attacked headquarters, the guards would certainly repel if not kill them. The agents would turn to flee, almost certainly to the port. Leaving at least a token contingent there would catch them in a pincer movement.

I'll take off the extras there and leave just the normal complement, she thought, disobeying her boss's orders. *If he criticizes me, I'll tell him I misunderstood his command.*

The trio from SOTE moved quietly on foot through the streets of Sanctuary. They dared not take the slow-moving carts now; to be caught in the open in one of those vehicles would be tantamount to suicide. So instead they skulked around the back streets or mingled in crowds traveling in the same direction.

They reached the gates of the spaceport by late afternoon and hid behind a building until the sun went down. Night would have to be their ally, although the spaceport field would not be completely dark. Floodlights would illuminate vast areas almost as brightly as day because, as dependent as Sanctuary was on its imported materials, the flow of incoming ships could not be abated for half the day simply because of a little darkness.

As they waited, the sharp eyes of Jules and Yvette scanned the field before them, trying to pick out all the guards and establish their routines.

"I'm nervous," Jules said as he surveyed the region ahead of them. "I don't see very many guards. They must know we're headed this way."

"I'd think that would make it easier," Helena said.

Yvette shook her head. "The guards you don't see are far more dangerous than the ones you do."

"Oh."

Nightfall came, however, and there was no sign of any more guards. Every second they delayed was another second in which they might be discovered, so Jules and Yvette agreed that, whether they knew the full layout or not, they would have to act now. Jules beckoned and the two women followed his lead.

Their first priority was to obtain weapons. They might be battling an army, and it would be an impossibility unless they themselves had guns. With this in mind, they crept up on a nearby tower where some sentries were stationed, away from the main body of the guard. These people would not be missed for a little while and, isolated as they were, they would make easy pickings.

Helena was left at the bottom of the tower to act as a lookout. Though the Head's Girl Friday was eager for action, the d'Alemberts impressed on her the special circumstances of this operation. They would have to climb up the outside of the tower and then still be prepared to fight at once. Space within the watchroom would be crowded; Jules and Yvette could fight as a coordinated unit, but adding a third member in such cramped quarters could be dangerous. Reluctantly, Helena agreed to stand at the base of the tower and whistle a warning if anything untoward should occur.

The two DesPlainians scrambled up opposite sides of the metal structure, grabbing at the guy wires and struts for handholds. They made no noise as they climbed; Helena occasionally glanced up and, even knowing they were there, she could not detect them. As much as she hated to admit it to herself, she would indeed have been a liability to them under these circumstances.

124

Jules and Yvette reached the top simultaneously and peered inside the open tower. There were only three men, grouped together at the center. They were entirely too relaxed, as though not expecting any trouble just yet. This worried Jules immensely; surely the bosses of Sanctuary would have realized that the SOTE trio would try to make their escape at the port. Why was security so lax?

At any rate, it was best to take advantage of the situation while it existed. Jules could see his sister's eyes across the way, and he managed to catch her attention. At a slight nod of his head, the DesPlainian furies leaped into action.

Vaulting over the enclosure, they waded into the group of sentries. Jules decked one man instantly with a roundhouse punch that connected solidly on the hapless fellow's jaw. Yvette gave her prime target a vicious blow to the kidneys, which doubled him over in pain and allowed her to finish him off with a hit on the back of the neck. She turned just in time to see Jules give the third man a kick in the solar plexus. The man gave a *whoosh* and backed almost directly into Yvette. The female agent spun him around and delivered the *coup de grâce* with a punch in the face. In less than five seconds, the d'Alemberts had captured the tower.

In bending over the guards to disarm them, the agents were surprised to find that the men were carrying only blasters. "They play for keeps, it seems," Yvette whispered, and Jules nodded solemnly. If the rest of the guards were similarly armed, they knew, their escape attempt would be a dangerous game indeed. Unfortunately for them it was the only game in town.

They scampered down the ladder again, and Jules handed Helena the third blaster they had captured. The Head's daughter took the weapon without comment, though she, too, must have realized the implications.

125

The trio then set off across the field toward a nearby ship that had recently unloaded and would be departing soon.

Because of Sanctuary's mild climate, many of the items taken off the vessels were left standing around outside at the edges of the field to await distribution, rather than being taken inside some warehouse. Consequently, what could have been an empty, flat plain between the gate and the ships was instead a veritable forest of boxes, crates, bins and other containers. These afforded some cover as the three agents crept forward so that, despite the bright floodlights that periodically swept the area, they managed to move along unseen.

Though they had thought the searchlights would be a hazard to overcome, the bright beams actually saved their lives. If it hadn't been for the illumination they provided, Yvette might never have caught sight of the guard party that was about to blast them out of existence.

They had made it to the front line of boxes, with nothing now between them and the ship they wanted but empty field. They discussed the matter quietly and decided to try to bridge the distance in one quick run between spotlight sweeps. They were waiting for this current sweep to end so they could make their break when Yvette's eye was attracted by a sudden glint to the left. The piercing intensity of the floodlight reflected off the belt buckle of one of the guards who had just walked into their row some twenty meters away. The guards had their blasters already drawn, and they spotted the intruders at almost precisely the same instant.

All stealth was cast aside now; their presence could no longer be kept secret. "Rube!" Yvette yelled to warn her brother, and at the same time moved into action herself. Helena could not be expected to react as quickly as a DesPlainian and, after all, the whole point

126

of their mission here had been to protect her and get her back safely to Earth. Therefore, Yvette's action was taken in Helena's direction. She leaped at the girl, brushing her rudely aside and into a small stack of crates, which toppled noisily to the ground.

At his sister's cry Jules, too, popped into instant action. He dived to his left—*toward* the attackers—simultaneously twisting his body in a squirming motion that was next to impossible to focus on. He hit the ground, with a crash that sent a tower of boxes cascading down on top of him. Although the impact of the boxes stunned him slightly, it was they, not himself, that took the brunt of the blaster fire that was pouring out of the sentries' guns. Some of the boxes were wooden and burst into flames as the heat from the weapons' beams brought them to the incineration point. Jules could feel the heat near his face and his eyebrows were slightly singed as he raised his own blaster and struggled out from under the pile to return the guards' fire.

He found himself facing a battery of three men and one woman, all firing at him without mercy. With a speed that only someone from a heavy-grav world could muster, he dodged through the conflicting beams, getting burned slightly in the process, until he found some metal boxes that offered him some cover. He fired back with his own weapon then, and one of the guards dropped immediately. The others, taking the warning, stopped their fire momentarily to head for cover themselves.

Jules took advantage of the respite—which lasted all of four seconds—to break away from his hiding place and bolt down the aisle at top speed . . . a speed that would leave a casual observer breathless. His enemies, though, had no time to be impressed; all they knew was that suddenly he was at the extreme limit of their blaster range and acting as a rapidly moving target. He would be impossible to hit under these conditions, so they would have to pursue him more actively. They darted from their shelters and took off in pursuit.

As he ran, Jules looked around to see if he could spot his sister or Helena. His hurried scan of the area revealed no sign of them. *Good,* he thought. Within minutes, the alarm about their presence here would be spread all over the city and every guard on Sanctuary would be converging on this area. If he could serve as a decoy to lead pursuit away from the other two, they might have a slightly better chance of getting away. He didn't even stop to think of what the consequences would be to himself; the success of the mission was his overriding consideration. In the longstanding tradition of d'Alembert loyalty, his own inevitable death meant little if it ultimately served the cause of Empire.

Yvette and Helena, meanwhile, had their own problems. The two had toppled into a stack of boxes at Yvette's initial leap. Helena, not expecting the sudden action, had had the wind knocked out of her lungs, but Yvette could not give her the time to recover. Every millisecond counted. Grabbing the other woman tightly by the wrist, Yvette dragged her friend hurriedly along the ground until they were behind another pile of crates.

The spotlight was off them for the moment and they were back in darkness, but that state of affairs would not last long. With all the noise this commotion was causing, it would only be a few seconds before the floodlights were focused steadily on this area. Yvette could hear the sounds of blasters in action. She assumed that her brother was keeping at least some of the sentries busy, but there might still be more of them searching the darkness for the two women. Their only chance for survival lay in rapid motion. They dared not stand still.

Helena was coughing and shaking her head dizzily.

Yvette yanked her roughly to her feet. "Come on," she whispered. "We can't stop now." And to herself she added, *You wanted a taste of field action; this should give you enough for your entire lifetime. Unfortunately, that may not be long.*

Helena made a valiant struggle and did manage to get to her feet. Her long black hair was all askew and covering half her face, so that she could barely see where she was going. Yvette led her along by the hand, slowing her own pace down to a comparative crawl. But it couldn't be helped; Helena had to be gotten out of here safely.

The floodlights swung on them again and sirens wailed through the night air. The sound drilled right through the women's skulls, rattling their thoughts. Yvette ceased planning her moves, relying on her well-trained instincts instead. If they couldn't save her, nothing could.

A silhouette appeared before her against the glare of the light. Yvette fired by reflex and the figure fell. More figures appeared to take its place. She pushed Helena violently sideways to get her out of the line of fire, and began an elaborate dance of her own to keep herself clear of the deadly beams.

Without warning, a wall of flames erupted on her left. Some of the boxes in that area must have contained combustible materials, and a searing blaster beam had ignited one pile. Within seconds, the area had heated up and was being covered by a cloud of thick, black smoke.

Yvette found herself choking on the fumes, but she was not alone—her pursuers were also caught in the sudden inferno. The coughing of smoke-filled throats assailed her ears, mingling with the hysteria of the sirens. She instinctively started running in the direction opposite the coughing, then realized Helena was not with her.

She looked around wildly, her eyes stinging from the smoke. Through the tears that were welling up, she thought she saw Helena being grabbed by one of the guards and dragged, kicking and biting, away. Then more guards closed in around the scene and cut it off from her further view.

She had to rescue Helena! That one thought resounded in her mind. But as she stopped and turned around to take a step in that direction, a stack of burning boxes toppled directly into her path, shooting sparks in all directions. The intense heat forced her back, and when she looked again Helena was gone.

Her instincts for survival came to the fore. If it was impossible, momentarily, to perform her mission, then she should save herself so that she could perform it later. She fled the confusion at the fire, blasting down the few stray guards she saw. There seemed to be more of them arriving every second, and the charge pack of her gun was beginning to fade out. She stopped beside the charred body of one of her would-be killers and traded guns with him; he would never miss it now.

The entire field was bathed in light now, and completely encircled by guards. She could hear them yelling back and forth at one another as they tried to coordinate their efforts to catch her. From the sounds of their voices, there must have been fifty of them.

For one of the few times in her life, Yvette felt the sinking feeling of despair. There did not seem to be any way in the Universe she could outfight and elude fifty fully armed people all by herself. Even she and her brother fighting back to back would have a hard time coping with odds of twenty-five to one—and enemy reinforcements were pouring in at an even greater rate.

It was not fear Yvette felt. She had long ago resigned

herself to the thought of dying in the service of her Emperor. What made her feel bad was the knowledge that she had failed in her mission here. To die and succeed was a glorious end; to die a failure was ignominious.

Suddenly she heard a thunderous roar, a squeal of tires and a crashing sound approaching her. From out of nowhere, a long, low limousine appeared. It was black, nearly five meters long and almost three wide. It came racing up at a breakneck pace, toppling stacks of crates that lay in its path.

It pulled to a screeching stop in front of her and one side door popped open. She raised her blaster to fire automatically, but some instinct made her hold back and not shoot. She thought she heard a voice over the din saying, "Quick, get in!"

There was absolutely nothing to lose at this point, so she did. The instant she was seated—before she could even close the door behind her—the car shot forward, knocking over still more cartons and adding to the total confusion.

The driver drove with such quick reflexes and reckless daring that she was sure it must be her brother. Her first glance at him through the semidarkness of the car's interior reinforced that impression. But then Yvette realized that she was making the same mistake she had made once before.

The person behind the controls was none other than Pias Nav.

CHAPTER 10

Interrogations

A thousand thoughts popped into Yvette's mind, a million questions that Nav had to answer occurred to her. She put all of them aside for the moment as irrelevant. Right now it didn't matter what heinous crimes Nav had committed; he was saving her from the guards, and that was what counted. Later, at a more convenient moment, questions of guilt could be raised.

Therefore, instead of thanking him or asking what he was doing here, her first words to him were, "My brother."

Nav understood precisely what she meant, and gave a slight nod. He pressed the accelerator button and the car gave an extra surge as it leaped forward on its new quest to find Jules. The presence of the car was confusing to the enemy. They knew it was one of their own vehicles, but it was behaving in a totally unexplained manner. A few of them guessed at the truth and fired blaster bolts in the car's direction. The few that hit bounced harmlessly off the metal sides; the car, Yvette surmised, must have enough armor plating to withstand the fire of hand weapons. But there were few shots that even came close to hitting; Nav was driving like a calculating madman, swerving in and out so quickly that few guards had time to react or take careful aim.

After driving recklessly for thirty seconds, they came to a cluster of guards gathered in one area and excited as a pack of hounds chasing a cornered animal. Jules had found a cargo tractor and had backed it up against the wall of a building. The tractor gave him effective cover to shoot at the guards while they had no clear shots at him. He could hold them at bay for the moment, but there was little doubt the charge in his blaster would soon be spent, leaving him stranded there helpless.

Nav drove at the pack of guards from the rear, where they weren't expecting an attack. They scattered quickly in their haste to avoid being run over, and Nav zipped through the crowd into no-man's-land, swerving broadside to a stop in front of Jules. Yvette flung her door and yelled, *"Ici!"*

Jules needed no second invitation. With one quick glance to make sure no one was in firing position at that instant, he vaulted over the tractor and crossed the distance between it and the car so rapidly that those people observing it could only blink in astonishment. Yvette slid over on the seat closer to Nav, giving her brother room to climb in beside her. As was the case before, Nav barely waited until Jules was in before gunning the accelerator to the limit. He spun the car around and headed for a little knot of guards who had started to regroup after his last pass. The people scattered again as Nav drove through and left a trail of havoc in his wake.

With no reason to linger now, Nav was not about to let anything stop him on his way out of the spaceport. He pushed his vehicle to its top speed of 175 kilometers an hour and was out the main gate before any of the guards could reach their own cars and give chase.

Garst was furious with himself. *I overestimated them this time,* he thought. *I thought that their being here meant they'd found out about me. But they hadn't. They were only investigating Sanctuary itself.*

He was grateful that he had a security chief like Rawling. If she had merely obeyed his orders, the SOTE trio would have gotten completely away, leaving him to look like an idiot while explaining the failure to Lady A. Rawling had behaved with commendable speed, too; at the first alarm from the port, she was able to mobilize nearly all her personnel and get them there on the double. It was solely through her efforts that Helena von Wilmenhorst had been captured intact. The two DesPlainians had escaped, but that was not Rawling's fault; no one could have presupposed the miraculous intervention of what had to be a fourth SOTE operative.

Rawling had apologized for that, of course, but she assured him that her people were combing the entire city and that no one could evade her net for long. Garst nodded, knowing just how thorough Rawling was.

I might as well examine my winnings. "Send in the von Wilmenhorst woman," he said aloud.

Helena was wheeled into the room. She had been strapped into a chair and, as a further precaution, had been given a mild tranquilizer to keep her from making any serious attempts to escape. But even the drug could not stifle the expression of shock that registered on her face as she saw him. Her eyebrows arched and she exclaimed *"Bozhe moi"* under her breath.

"Do you recognize me then, Your Grace?" Garst asked, using her formal title to indicate he knew who she was.

"I . . . I've seen pictures. You're Garst. But . . . but you're dead."

"An exaggerated but convenient rumor. No doubt your DesPlainian friends described my demise in some detail."

134

Helena did not react to that remark, so Garst continued his harangue. "Well, it is true that, when I saw the woman charging at me, I started running. My foot slipped and I fell through the door to the vat of recycling chemicals. There is, however, a catwalk for the benefit of the plant's workers that runs around the lip of the tank; I landed on that and ran around to the tank's back exit before anyone came to the door to look in. When they couldn't see me, they surmised I had fallen into the chemicals and been dissolved. I saw no profit in disillusioning them. Instead, I left Vesa as quickly as I could and made some contacts that eventually landed me in charge of the operation here."

He walked over to the helpless woman, pulled up a chair and sat down next to her. "Now that I've been so gracious as to tell you some things about myself, perhaps you would care to reciprocate. What are you doing here?"

Helena just glared at him.

"I know you are Duchess Helena von Wilmenhorst, chief administrative assistant to your father the Grand Duke, who is also the Head of SOTE."

Helena's eyes widened, but still she said nothing.

"But there still are so many things I don't know, and I need to know them. Who your friends are, for instance, and what I may expect from them. But you're not going to tell me, are you?"

More silence from the girl strapped in the chair.

Garst sighed and stood up. "I didn't really think you would. SOTE personnel have a high reputation for not divulging information willingly, even under torture. It's even said that they are given conditioning against most forms of truth drugs. Which leaves me only one alternative."

He went to his desk and, out of the top drawer, pulled a hyposprayer filled with a colorless liquid.

There was no doubt in Helena's mind what that fluid was: nitrobarb. Under its influence, she would tell Garst anything he wanted to know—and she only had a fifty percent chance of surviving the experience, even if Garst decided to let her live.

"Don't use that," she said. "I'll talk."

"A very nice offer, Your Grace—but at this stage of our relationship, not a very trustworthy one. You would talk most fluently and most dishonestly, giving me lies that are backed up with just enough truth to make them believable. I think I'll stick to proven methods."

As he approached the bound girl, she struggled to get away, but to no avail. Garst injected the vicious drug into her arm and within seconds she had passed into the deep coma that was the first step of the drug's reaction. In another twenty minutes she would return to semi-consciousness and tell him anything that was in her mind.

Garst settled back patiently to wait, suddenly feeling very confident. He had plenty of time.

The three fugitives ditched their stolen car shortly after they'd escaped from the spaceport area and eluded their pursuit. Since all three were from heavy gravity worlds, they were able to run at an equal pace and be far enough away from the car to be safe—for a short while at least.

They took refuge in an alley behind a group of stores that were closed for the night. There in the shadows they bent over, panting to recover their breath before deciding what move to make next. Jules in particular was very concerned about this sudden turn of events and what it might mean. He had not questioned Nav before now because, like Yvette, he knew their main hope lay in running as fast as possible. But now that

136

they were momentarily out of danger, there were a few things he wanted to know.

"I want to thank you for saving both our lives, of course," he began, "but I have to know what in the Galaxy you were doing out there."

"I don't suppose you'd believe I was just in the neighborhood and saw your light," Nav said, flashing an ingenuous smile. Jules did not react, and Nav's smile faded. "*Khorosho*, I'll tell you the truth. I was getting a little tired of this planet and I wanted to be moving on. Some of my Gypsy heritage, I guess. I was outside the spaceport field, trying to decide how best to get in, when all of a sudden everything in there exploded. I saw the two of you in trouble, and thought I'd help."

"Just out of the goodness of your heart, is that it?" Jules sneered.

"It was mostly for your sister's sake," the gambler shot back. "I feel a great deal of . . . well, interest in her welfare."

Jules snorted and Yvette looked sadly away so that Nav would not see the look in her eyes.

"What is it with you two? I've just saved your lives and instead of being grateful, you start criticizing me. Has it occurred to you that I'm now in a good deal of trouble too, because of that? What do you expect from me?"

Jules looked him straight in the eye. "How about a little truth for a change?"

It was the Newforester's turn to avert his gaze. "What do you mean?"

"I mean that your name is not really Pias Nav," Jules began. "The initials on your handkerchief are PB."

"I have a lot of enemies. Necessity sometimes requires . . ."

137

"And I saw what you did to Rowe Carnery." Jules's voice was icy cold as he uttered those words.

A silence hung in the air for ten seconds. The muscles in Nav's throat tightened, and his fists clenched and unclenched several times. Finally he turned his back on the two of them. "I don't owe any explanations to a couple of cat burglars," he said harshly.

Yvette reached out, grabbed him by one arm and spun him around to face her. Backing him up against the wall, she said, "What about me? Do you owe an explanation to *me*?"

The two of them stood there, frozen, for what seemed like seven eternities. Their eyes were locked, the expressions on their faces were totally unreadable. It was Nav who backed down first. His shoulders sagged and he stared down at his feet. "*Khorosho,* Yarmilla," he said in a voice not much above a whisper. "Just for you."

He seated himself on the edge of a trash bin. "You're right about my name—half right, at least. My first name is Pias, but the last name is Bavol. I am indeed from Newforest, but until a couple of years ago I wasn't primarily a gambler. I might never even have left Newforest if it weren't for Rowe Carnery.

"I was engaged at the time to a beautiful girl named Miri. I won't bore you by telling you how much I loved her; it was a lot. Miri was returning to Newforest after visiting Appeny. She had a considerable fortune in jewels along with her, which she kept in a personal safe that had been specially installed in her cabin. She was the only person aboard who knew how to open it.

"Pirates boarded her ship just before it reached Newforest. They knew they had less than an hour to make their haul before entering Newforest's space and risking an encounter with the Imperial Navy. They killed the captain outright when he swore he didn't know how to open the safe. Miri wasn't so lucky.

"They . . . questioned her; that's the kindest way I can put it. Miri always was a stubborn woman; she refused to talk. The pirates were in a hurry, and they used very crude but painful tortures. Eventually they had to give up and flee when the Navy boarded the ship, and Miri still had her jewels—for all the good they did her."

The Newforester's fists were clenched, his eyes tightly closed. His breathing was jagged, and it seemed an effort to speak. Beads of perspiration stood out on his forehead.

"I couldn't begin to describe what was done to her. It was horrible. They took her back to a hospital on Newforest and wouldn't let me see her until they'd cleaned up the worst of the blood, but even so . . . even so . . ." He choked on the words and had to pause for a few minutes until he could get himself more under control.

"She took three days dying. I was beside her almost all the time. I didn't eat anything. I drank occasional glasses of some liquid they put into my hand, but I don't know what it was. They had her doped up to her earlobes with painkillers, but they couldn't ease the agony in her mind. Every time I looked into her eyes I could see the horror, the pain, the . . ."

He broke down completely at this point and began sobbing. Instinctively, Yvette moved over to him. She put her arms around him and held onto him tightly. Pias Bavol buried his face in her bosom and wept openly and unashamed for several minutes as Yvette tenderly stroked his hair and made soft, cooing noises. Jules stood to one side, feeling very much an intruder in this scene.

At length Bavol pulled his head back. "I must apologize," he said hoarsely. "I've been holding that in for so long, and now . . ."

"I understand," Yvette soothed. "Just go on with your story when you can."

Bavol wiped at his eyes with his sleeve, and after a few seconds got his voice under control. "She did have a few lucid moments, and she described the pirate leader fairly well. She mentioned a pendant he wore on a silver chain around his neck; she described it in detail. After she . . . she died, I swore to avenge her death. Remember, I told you we've very protective of our women on Newforest. This pirate had committed an unpardonable sin and caused immense suffering and death to someone I loved. I dedicated my life to returning the favor.

"I left my home and started tracking down this monster on my own. It didn't take me long to learn his name—Rowe Carnery—but getting close to him was another matter. I adopted the personality of Pias Nav, itinerant gambler and layabout; it suited my personality anyway, and I found that people would talk more openly to me if I appeared to be part of their milieu.

"Carnery moved around a lot from planet to planet, which was one reason why he was so hard to catch. I tracked right along after him, without his ever knowing I was on his trail. Finally we got to Cordoba; just when I was about to close in, he opted to come here to Sanctuary. I had no choice but to come along. I didn't dare kill him aboard the ship; there would have been too few suspects, and I would probably have been found out. Here there were a lot more people, and I had a better chance to escape undetected." He paused and looked straight at Jules. "But I swear to you, Carnery was the only person I've ever killed in my entire life. I don't regret it, either. Nothing can make me feel sorry for what I did to that bastard—not after the butcher job he did on Miri."

"Wait a minute," Jules said. "You told us aboard ship that you killed someone on Cordoba and had to get

140

off the planet in a hurry. That was why you came to Sanctuary."

Bavol smiled sheepishly. "I lied, there. When I found that Carnery was coming to Sanctuary, I knew I'd have to get myself into some trouble before I'd be allowed along. I followed a pair of blasterbats who worked for one casino owner, and watched them kill someone who'd welched on a bet. Then I framed myself for the murder, leaving my fingerprints and enough clues that the police would think I'd done it. That was my credential to get aboard. I've told you so many lies in the past you may not believe what I've just said, but it's the truth, I swear it."

Yvette looked at him solemnly. "I believe it." Then she turned to her brother. The expression on her face dared him to contradict her.

Jules took his time deciding. Bavol's explanation was a logical one. It explained the murder, the expression on the Newforester's face in Carnery's cabin, and all the other discrepancies in the man's behavior. The emotional outburst Bavol had just displayed was genuine, Jules was sure of that. And while he could not condone Carnery's murder in so grotesque and bloody a fashion, Jules could not exactly condemn Bavol for it either; under those circumstances, he might have done the same thing himself. He imagined someone doing that to his own fiancée, Vonnie Roumenier, and he shivered.

Besides, Bavol had risked his own life to save theirs. That ought to count for something. "*Khorosho*," Jules nodded, "I believe you."

"There's something I'd like to get clear myself," Bavol said. "Now that we've gotten my identity straightened around, what about yours? From all the things you've been doing, from this terrible grilling you've been putting me through, I have the definite feeling the two of you are not just burglars."

141

"We *are* the cat burglars the police on Cordoba were looking for," Yvette said, hedging the issue.

"But that's not your full occupation, is it?"

Jules had to hand it to Bavol; the man was no fool. "I'm afraid we can't say anything more about it for the time being."

Bavol looked to Yvette, who just shook her head. "Please don't ask," she said.

The Newforester shrugged his shoulders. "Then for the moment I'm a gambler and you're a pair of cat burglars—and all of us are running in fear of our lives. We can't sit here too much longer without being discovered, so I presume we must either make some plans to hide or get ourselves off this planet as soon as possible."

Yvette shook her head. "There's something else we have to do before we can leave. A friend of ours is in trouble."

"Yes, I saw her with you for a while during your fight."

"We have to either bring her with us or know for a fact that she's dead."

Bavol gave a low whistle. "That's going to take some doing. You don't happen to have a small army tucked in your pockets, do you?"

Jules put a hand on the other man's shoulder. "This isn't your fight, you know. You've already done more for us than we have any right to expect. You're free to walk away and take your chances on your own."

Bavol shook his head. "It's too late for that now. The guards will think I'm with you, so they'll be hunting me just as strenuously. Our fates are linked together for better or worse," he said, looking particularly at Yvette. Then, with a wry grin, he added, "Till death do us part, apparently."

"Welcome to our team, then," Jules said, and got down to business. "The odds are that they'll be keeping

142

Hel . . . our friend at the safest place they've got, which will be their headquarters. They know we'll be coming after her, so they can set up their defenses as tightly as they know how."

"Do you have any idea where their headquarters is?" Bavol asked.

"We think so," Yvette replied. "The address we were given is 666 Crowley Drive. That should be the first place we check."

"I agree," Jules said. "And we'd better do it soon, because we won't stand any chance if they catch us flat-footed in this alley. Our best hope lies in being mobile, so let's get moving."

CHAPTER 11

Playing With Fire

Garst was literally stunned by the gold mine of information he was able to extract from the hapless Helena. The more he probed, the more he learned about the innermost secrets of the Service of the Empire. It made him respect SOTE even more than he had—and it made him hungry to start some plans of his own.

Imagine using the Circus of the Galaxy to get your best agents onto any planet you wished, he thought. *The talents of the d'Alembert family must be incredible— and particularly this Jules and Yvette. No wonder they've behaved so spectacularly. But they're not invincible. If I hadn't acted so foolishly I could have killed them earlier tonight.*

But it was no matter, he knew. As long as he had the von Wilmenhorst woman, they would come to him. They would pick their own particular time, but he could choose the battleground for this particular fight—and it would be here, in the nerve center of his entire operation, where he was surrounded by guards and foolproof defenses. Let them come, he was ready for them.

Helena was slumped over in her chair after nearly two hours of fruitful interrogation. She was in a coma that would last for at least twenty hours. This was the last stage of the effects of nitrobarb. Either she would emerge from her coma at the end of that period or she would slip into a quiet death. Garst hoped she would live—she might still have some uses—but he would not shed any tears if she died.

He stood up from his own chair and stretched his legs, which were stiff from sitting so long. He had important things to think about. Although Lady A had told him her organization knew virtually everything SOTE did, he had strong doubts that she knew about the d'Alemberts and the Circus. According to Helena, that information was so secret that it had never been written down or put into computer records; it went purely by word of mouth, and only a few top people in SOTE—plus, of course, the Imperial Family—were privy to that information.

This meant he held a vital key that the others didn't even know existed. Knowledge, he knew, is power. By rights, he should have placed a call immediately to Earth to alert Lady A of his new findings. He didn't have her exact com number; he would, as always, have to leave a message with an impersonal machine and she would call him back at her convenience. That, she said, was so that if he were captured he wouldn't be able to lead anyone to her. He suspected, though, that she also wished to maintain the social distance between them; familiarity, so the theory went, bred contempt.

But, as the thought of Lady A fled through his mind, he knew he was not going to tell her of his discovery. If she was going to keep secrets from him, it was only right that he keep a few from her. There had to be some way he could capitalize on his new knowledge, and it would only take him a little time to think of it.

But those were thoughts for the future. He forced his mind back to concentrate on the here and now. Jules and Yvette d'Alembert were still loose somewhere on Sanctuary, along with their mysterious ally whom even Helena didn't know. Three people, two of whom were the top SOTE agents in the entire Galaxy and one of whom was a total unknown. But even if his skills were some-how equal to the d'Alemberts—he certainly couldn't be better—that still would leave them hopelessly out-classed. Even after the debacle at the spaceport, Garst still had over a hundred guards in his security force. That was more than enough to deal with only three peo-ple.

He buzzed the intercom for Rawling. When her face lit up in his screen, he asked, "What's the guard deploy-ment?"

"I've got a double shift working the port, a double shift standing sentry here in HQ and the rest out on a search pattern."

"Pull in the search teams. Our friends will have to come to us if they want to get the girl, which they do. We should concentrate rather than disperse our forces."

"*Khorosho*." Rawling jotted down the order on a piece of paper. "Anything else, sir?"

"Yes, take off all the exterior guards from this com-plex."

"Sir?" The security chief's tone was clearly dubious.

"We don't want to discourage them; we want them to come in. A good trap should be like a spiderweb—very easy to fly into and very, very difficult to leave."

"Smooth, sir. I'll get on it right away."

The d'Alemberts and their new ally made their way cautiously through the back streets of the city toward the address Helena had given them. As she'd indicated, it was near the spaceport, back in the direction from which they'd come. They met with no resistance as they moved, a fact that made Jules distinctly edgy.

The building at that address was a low, flat white structure, flanked by several others just like it. Its front was almost forty meters across, and it seemed to extend for hundreds of meters away from the street. There was a chain link fence around the building only one and a half meters high, and a yard five meters wide before the wall of the building. The front facade was absolutely bare except for the numbers 666 right beside the door. There was just the one portal, and it was only wide enough for one person at a time to enter. There was no sign of any windows anywhere around the outside of the building.

"Getting in is going to be a bit of a problem," Jules said. "We can't just walk in there one by one; we'll be blasted where we stand, without a chance to fight back."

"Maybe there's a copter entrance on the roof," Bavol suggested.

"Perhaps, but the area's so well lighted we'd never get across it without being spotted," Jules said.

"There's got to be more than that," Yvette spoke up. "What if there's an emergency? There has to be some way of getting people into and out of there in large numbers, otherwise the design is inefficient. And whoever planned this setup is far from inefficient."

"Well, I can't see anything that looks even remotely like that," Bavol complained.

They were all silent for a moment as they strained their eyes against the darkness of night to make out details on the building. Finally, Yvette spoke up again. "Speaking of seeing things, we've been here for several days and I don't recall ever seeing any cars like the one you rescued us in—nothing but those damned carts that only go fifteen kilometers an hour. Where did you find that thing, anyway?"

"Some guards drove up in it and climbed out, leaving it empty and ready for the taking," Bavol explained. "I don't know where they came from, and I wasn't about to question that particular gift horse—not when it was needed so badly at the time."

147

"The streets aren't really built to accommodate them," said Jules. "It's pointless to use sleek machines like those on the same avenues the carts are on; the carts would slow them down to a crawl. Again, it would be inefficient."

"So," Yvette continued the line of reasoning, "there would have to be special roadways where the black cars can travel by themselves, unhindered."

"I haven't seen any trace of that," the Newforester pointed out.

"Exactly," exclaimed Yvette with enthusiasm. "Which means that they've been placed where no one will see them."

"Underground?" Jules asked.

Yvette nodded. "That's my guess."

"I can imagine it—a whole series of interconnected roads under the surface of the city itself, radiating out like spokes from a wheel—probably with this headquarters building as the hub." Jules was catching his sister's enthusiasm for this theory.

"With arcs crisscrossing the radii at intervals. And there would be nodes or special access points to the surface, well disguised up here. That way a squad of guards could be dispatched from headquarters to anyplace in the city in a matter of minutes and seem to appear from nowhere."

"Is it possible to do all that underground?" Bavol asked.

"You've obviously never been to Vesa or you wouldn't ask that question. That entire moon is honeycombed under the surface with tunnels and caverns. The technology has been in existence for centuries. Where have you been hiding?"

"Newforest," Bavol said abashedly. "We're a bit provincial there, I'm told."

Jules was becoming impatient. "The best plan of attack," he began, "is to ignore this door. It's certain death to go in there. But with an underground labyrinth as complex as theirs must be, they couldn't possibly guard all the routes at once. We'll find some way to slip in."

"As soon as we find an entranceway to the underground system," Yvette pointed out.

"But even if we get in, they'll have a thick cordon of guards all around your friend," Bavol said. "We won't be able to penetrate that wall."

"We can take care of both problems at one and the same time," Jules said with confidence. "I have a plan."

Half an hour later, the alarm bells began ringing in the security office and throughout the headquarters complex. Jinda Rawling flipped several switches on her desktop console to find out what the cause was. At almost the same instant, Garst buzzed for her on the intercom. She was perfectly capable of handling both situations at once; even as she continued to seek the information, she was responding to her boss. "Yes, sir?"

"What in hell is happening?"

"Just a second, sir." The information came through as she was speaking. "Let's see—fires have broken out in three different apartment buildings, all widely scattered."

"Three, eh? That's a very convenient number. It looks like our friends are trying their hands at arson as well as mayhem."

"Yes, sir. I'll send out the fire units."

"No."

"But sir . . ."

"We can't send out anyone. That's what they want us to do, dilute our forces down here so they can attack. We have to remain strong if we're going to win."

"But the clients . . ."

"Will just have to take care of themselves. This is far more important."

Rawling snapped off with a bitter "Yes, sir" and broke the intercom circuit. She didn't know what to think, except that it was very obvious her superior had a monomania on the subject of those agents out there.

Fifteen minutes later, three more fires started. Then three more. Then three more. Rawling buzzed Garst's office. "Sir, we've *got* to do something about those fires."

"Absolutely not. We cannot weaken security at headquarters."

Rawling lost her temper. "Begging your pardon, sir," she said in a cold fury, "but what in hell good does it do to protect headquarters if the whole drapping city burns to the ground?"

"We need to make those agents come to us and we need to stop them dead. It's vitally important."

"Please tell me what's so important. I'm dying to know."

Garst did not dare confide in the woman that he knew these agents were SOTE's top operatives; he knew she would tell Lady A at the first opportunity, and his monopoly on the knowledge would evaporate. "The deaths of those people will be, in the long run, far more important than a dozen Sanctuaries."

"But why, sir?" Rawling reiterated.

It was Garst's turn to lose his temper. "Because I gave you a direct order, that's why. If you won't obey it, I'll find someone who will." And he clicked off the intercom.

The security chief sat staring at the blank screen for thirty seconds, trying to make some sense out of her boss's orders. She finally came to the conclusion that they made no sense; on the subject of those SOTE agents, her boss was simply not sane. He could not make an objective decision. No three people could be special enough to risk the destruction of an entire city in order to ensure their deaths.

I was hired to be security chief of this entire planet, she thought. *It would be a betrayal of my responsibility to let the city be burned to the ground on the whims of a madman.* She had disobeyed a direct order earlier that evening, and had saved the day because of it; it looked as though she would have to do the same thing again.

Reaching for her microphone, she broadcast orders to her troops. Two squads were to remain on duty in central, with orders to kill the intruders on sight. One shift was to remain on duty at the port. The rest of her people were to take the fire-fighting equipment and go out to battle the blazes that were erupting all over the city.

As an afterthought, she decided to go out on the guard lines herself, so that she would be away from her desk and Garst couldn't reach her as easily. As far as she was concerned, the man—who had proven himself quite capable before today—had suddenly turned into a raging creature of unreason. She made a mental note to report his behavior to Lady A at the first opportunity.

Two squads should be perfectly capable of defending this place against three people, she thought as she strapped on her blaster and strode rapidly out of the office.

Up on the surface, pandemonium would have been too gentle a word to describe what was happening.

The fires started by the d'Alemberts and Pias Bavol were all in residential apartments, where the majority of Sanctuary's inhabitants could be found at this time of night. While the buildings did have automatic machinery to take care of small fires, the d'Alemberts had been trained in some tricks of the incendiary trade, and were able to quickly explain them to their ally. As a result, these fires were stubborn ones, and would not be quelled by automatic machinery. Soon whole buildings were ablaze, and the residents were fleeing to the streets for their lives.

When no guards appeared to fight the fires, more were set, and still more. "They have to come out sometime," Jules reasoned, "or they won't have anything left to defend."

Other buildings near the torched ones also caught fire and within an hour it seemed as though half the city were ablaze. The "citizenry" of Sanctuary milled about in the streets; no procedure had ever been established whereby they could call for help, and they were totally mystified that the people responsible for their welfare were not doing anything to assist them. Their confusion quickly turned to anger and resentment; they had paid enormous sums of money to come here, and now they were endangered for no apparent reason. The subliminal tension of Sanctuary was rapidly rising to the surface.

Jules and Yvette decided to help the chaos along by running through the mob and yelling, "Why won't they help us? We paid them, why don't they protect us from things like this?"

That tactic seemed to work even better than they had expected. The two supersiblings conferred for a moment and agreed that this was a diversion that should be used to the fullest advantage. They looked for, and eventually found, Pias Bavol and explained their plan to him.

"Let's really give the guards something to worry about," Yvette said, having to shout to be heard above the din in the streets. "You're good with words, and the authorities never really got a good look at you as our helper. You stir the people up and lead them in an attack against the headquarters building on the surface

152

level. They won't shoot you on sight like they would us. While we're working on the underground levels, you can keep them busy up top."

"Confusion to our enemies," Pias nodded with a smile.

Yvette touched him lightly on the arm. "Don't be in the front lines yourself," she added privately. "It's beginning to look as though we might survive this escapade after all, and I'd hate to have you be one of the casualties."

"Don't worry, I'm a confirmed coward," he said. He kissed her lightly on the forehead and raced off to begin his new task.

Jules watched him go. "We need more cowards like that," he said, mostly to himself. Yvette heard him, though, and smiled inwardly.

The guards began arriving several minutes later. They were quite surprised to discover that they had to contend with not just the fires, but with the irate citizens as well. As they tried to maneuver their equipment into position to fight the flames, they found themselves pelted with rocks, pieces of rubble and any other loose objects the angry inhabitants could find. Pias was doing his job well, feeding the fires of resentment and stirring the crowd to a fever pitch. When he suggested an attack on headquarters itself, it became a battle cry that echoed through the streets of Sanctuary.

Yvette and Jules, meanwhile, were paying very close attention to the guards. The firefighting equipment was big and bulky, and had to be moved slowly into position. Consequently, the d'Alemberts were able to trace easily where the machines were coming from. There were big structures that looked like office buildings from the front, but were actually just false facades; the entire back end could swing out to allow cars, people or firetrucks to pass through.

The two superagents waited near one of these entrances until all the personnel and equipment had emerged. As the large door slid automatically shut, they dodged inside unseen and found themselves at the top of a broad ramp. The slope at their feet went down for fifteen meters before leveling off into a wide, well lit corridor.

There were three of the long black cars parked at the foot of the ramp, and two men stood guard over them. It was obvious they were not expecting any trouble— they were talking casually to one another, not even looking in the direction of the ramp. Their blasters were tucked securely into their holsters.

Jules and Yvette slipped down the ramp quietly, hugging tightly against the wall to attract minimum attention. By the time one of the guards happened to look up and see their movement, it was far too late for him or his partner to do anything about it.

Two flying DesPlainian forms came at them before they could even reach for their guns. Yvette's victim got a simple blow to the chin knocking him unconscious; Jules's took a little more persuading. A knee to the breadbasket and an open-handed chop to the throat, however, put him out of commission.

The agents scrambled into the nearest car, with Jules in the driver's seat. The car surged ahead down the high-ceilinged corridor toward the headquarters building—and the agents' last chance to rescue Helena.

CHAPTER 12

Sortie On Sanctuary

They encountered no opposition as they rode along—but then, they had expected none. All free hands would doubtless be busy battling both the blaze and the rioters overhead. The core guard group would be closely clustered around command central.

Jules drove until he could see a major terminal coming up about a hundred meters further on. Stopping the car, he said, "I think we'd better walk from here. We'll have less protection but more mobility."

Yvette concurred and got out of the car. Together the two agents loped down the corridor at a deceptively fast pace until they came to the edge of an intersection. There, under a large vaulted dome, was a wide wooden doorway with three guards standing in front of it and a guard on either side encased in a blaster-proof booth. The booths were mounted with external weapons so that the sentries inside could fire out without being vulnerable themselves.

"We could cut down the three at the door from here," Yvette whispered, "but those two in the booths are going to be a problem. We can't get at them."

"We don't have to get *at* them," Jules responded. "We just have to get *by* them. Let's go back to the car, I've got an idea."

They jogged back down the corridor to their vehicle.

As they climbed inside, Jules said, "You take care of the three front guards, then hold on tight."

He backed the car down the tunnel for half a kilometer to allow him room to build up speed. Then, with full acceleration, he gunned the car forward toward the headquarter entrance.

They burst into the cavern at a speed in excess of a hundred and fifty kilometers an hour. They were on top of the guards before the latter knew what was happening. It took all the speed of Yvette's DesPlainian reflexes to fire at her targets in so short a time—but fire she did. All three of the exterior guards fell to the ground, victims of her deadly blaster.

Jules made no attempt to decelerate. With the car moving as quickly as he could make it, they rammed full tilt into the front doors of the entranceway. The crash jolted both of them down to the base of their teeth, but they were prepared for it and were properly braced. The massive machine hit the heavy doors and went through them as though they were made of cheap plywood. The car stalled and died completely as it shattered the portals, but it had accomplished the task Jules had set for it.

Quickly the two agents climbed out the doors and picked their way forward over the crumpled hood of the car. The beam-proof booths in which the two guards were stationed had not been designed to be defended from the rear, and the guards inside knew it. They had personal blasters of their own, but not enough time to use them as the d'Alemberts split and came after them at inconceivable speeds. Rather than killing the guards with their blasters, Jules and Yvette chose—independently of one another—to merely incapacitate them. With the swiftness of their reflexes, they were able to knock the guards unconscious with a single powerful blow apiece.

The breaking in of the doors had started alarm bells ringing all through the underground complex, but it would take several seconds for the rest of the security staff to realize what sector the danger was coming from and to mobilize their defenses. These were seconds that the d'Alemberts could—and did—use to their utmost advantage. The hallway that stretched before them was seventy meters long; they covered the distance in about five seconds, and met with no opposition in that time. There were some more closed doors at the end, but no guards stood outside. To Jules and Yvette, that only meant that the guards were inside the door, waiting for them.

The doors were constructed to open outward, toward them. Relying on the swiftness of their reflexes to give them an edge over anyone inside, the two agents yanked the doors outward and raced inside. There, they found five more guards waiting for them. The defenders all had their weapons drawn and prepared to fire, but the pair of DesPlainian hurricanes did not offer easy targets.

Yvette knocked out one guard, a woman, with a solid punch to the jaw, then went after a second. Jules, meanwhile, had picked up one man and hurled him bodily at another opponent. The force of the impact as the two collided left them both panting deeply on the floor, unable to take part in further action for some time to come. If Jules had had a stun-gun with him instead of a blaster, he would have shot the two to keep them out of commission for a while; but the thought of slaughtering the two helpless guards—even though he knew they'd do it to him if they had a chance—was repugnant to him. By the time they could recover sufficiently to be any threat to him, the battle would probably be decided anyway, so he left them as they were and concentrated on the rest of the opposition.

Yvette had planted one fist solidly in the stomach of a fourth guard and, as he doubled over, she used her other fist to make sure he gave her no further trouble. She whirled around, looking for the fifth person who had been standing guard inside the door, and found herself staring down the barrel of a powerful blaster.

Before that weapon could be fired, however, Jules swung into action. His right foot kicked out in one rapid motion and knocked the weapon forcefully out of the hand of the woman aiming it at his sister. The momentum of his leap brought him down on his left foot in front of the woman. He made a complete spin around and was prepared to knock her out totally when he noticed an insignia on her uniform indicating that she was the chief security officer. She could be more useful to them awake than unconscious. So instead he altered his motion and grabbed her around the neck in the crook of his right elbow.

The woman—whose name, Rawling, was stenciled above her left breast—knew how to handle herself. Instinctively she gave Jules a judo flip that sent him flying across the room. But that left her in an exposed position, and Yvette finished her off with an open-handed blow to the kidneys that left the security chief gasping and retching on the floor of the corridor.

Jules fell perfectly and rolled to his feet, only to find that his sister had taken care of the menace. From the grin Yvette shot him, he knew it would take him a while to live down the fact that he'd let himself be thrown like a novice instead of blocking the move like an experienced professional. But not a word was said now; there was still too much danger, and too much to do.

He ran back to the gagging woman, grabbed her by the top of her hair and yanked her roughly to her feet. "You're holding a friend of ours," he said. "We want her back."

"I . . . don't know what you're talking about," Rawling gasped.

Yvette grabbed the woman's arm and twisted it behind the security chief's back. "I've noticed," she said, "that memory restoration is in direct proportion to pain applied. I can break everything you've got unless you tell me."

"She's in . . . main office."

"That's a little better. Now, would you like to lead us there—notifying us, of course, of any boobytraps along the way?" Yvette nodded to her brother as she spoke and Jules let go of the woman's head.

Rawling nearly fell, but managed to catch herself and maintain some of her dignity. Her throat was still sore and she was choking, but she was able to glare defiantly at her two captors, each of whom had a blaster trained directly on her. "You don't have a prayer," she said.

"Then that puts us in good company with you. I'm told that a person can still walk and talk with a missing left arm, so if you want to keep yours you can start moving. Now!" Yvette's tone of voice left no room for argument.

Rawling had little choice but to comply. She was a wise enough woman to realize that anything was preferable to the certain death she would face at the hands of these two DesPlainians if she should disobey them. Even if this entire organization were broken up and she was forced to stand trial, her own crimes were not major enough to merit a serious sentence. Better to play the odds and hope for a chance to make her break later. "All right," she gritted. "This way."

From a doorway further on, three more guards emerged, guns drawn. They saw the d'Alemberts, whom they'd been ordered to kill on sight, and their first impulse was to fire; but then they saw their chief standing in front of the targets, and they were not sure what to do. As they stood there hesitating, Jules said quietly to Rawling, "We don't enjoy killing people. This doesn't have to be a bloodbath. The choice is yours."

Just then they heard a loud noise over their heads, and the sound of a low roar and lots of scuffling. "Sounds like the reinforcements," Yvette commented, adding for Rawling's benefit, "We invited a few more people to join the party. Your guards could really spend their time better by seeing that the rioters don't get out of hand."

The security chief had no desire to die in a crossfire. "Keep the people in line upstairs," she snapped at her men. "That's an order." The guards were obviously hesitant about leaving their leader in such a predicament, but there was nothing else they could do to help her. Besides, their help *was* needed upstairs to cope with the swarms of rioters who were currently rampaging through the corridors. Silently, they turned and left, and the d'Alemberts breathed a mutual sigh of relief that their captive was a reasonable woman.

"Now," Yvette said to Rawling, "I believe you were about to take us somewhere."

The uniformed woman led them down the hall to one particular door, then stepped through. The other two followed after her. Rawling had tried to use the opportunity to run away, but a blast from Yvette's gun landing just centimeters in front of her feet brought her to a screeching halt. "Not quite so fast," Yvette said. "We'd like to keep up with you." Rawling waited until the pair caught up with her, then continued.

She led them down a maze of hallways, and the d'Alemberts realized how lucky they'd been to capture her. It might have taken them forever to find their way through this labyrinth unassisted.

A couple of times they ran into more of Rawling's guards, but each time the security chief was able to order the men upstairs to quell the riot. From the sounds that were emanating over their heads, the guards were having a singular lack of success. Pias Bavol was performing his job admirably well.

They came to one door and Rawling hesitated as she reached for the knob. "Go ahead," Jules said. "You go first."

"I can't," the woman said. "That room is booby-trapped."

"How?"

"The knob is wired for electricity—and even if it should be opened, a blaster is trained on the door and kills anyone standing in front of it."

"Can't it be turned off?" Yvette asked.

"Yes, but I don't have the key. Garst does."

Garst? That was the first time the SOTE operatives had heard that name in connection with this case. Jules looked at his sister, and saw a shocked experession on her face. "Then Garst is in charge of this place?" he asked Rawling.

"Yes, for the past three months."

Jules was confused; he was sure he'd seen the head of the Vesan murder ring fall into a recycling vat and die. His sister also appeared puzzled, but an expression was beginning to form on her face that Jules had seen there only once before—when she had stood at the door to the vat, looking down into the seething chemicals. It was a mixture of horror, hatred, anger, and . . . what? Jules doubted even Yvette knew for certain what she was feeling.

Evidently, though, Garst had somehow survived that ordeal and come here secretly, to head up this new criminal endeavor. Jules put aside such speculations as hopeless; right now, the time was for action. In particular, he had to drag his sister out of the morass of emotions she was experiencing. Later, when this whole affair was over, they could wonder how Garst got here. It was only important now that he *was* here.

"Is there any way to get through other than this door?" Jules asked their captive.

Rawling shook her head. "Not on this level. You'd have to go all the way up to the surface and go around to the other side."

"And by that time," Jules reasoned, "anything could happen. All right, stand back—we'll see how effective this boobytrap is."

The three of them stood well to either side, and the two agents focused their blasters on the hinges of the wooden door. The metal hardware began to melt under the constant searing heat and, after a minute, the door fell in of its own weight. The falling of the door broke an electrical connection, and suddenly a continuous blaster beam flashed out through the opening, waist-high. Anyone standing in the doorway would have been sliced in half.

"Looks passable to me," Jules commented after studying the setup for a moment. "*Khorosho,* Rawling, after you."

"But I can't walk through that, I'll be killed."

"Nobody said 'walk,'" Yvette spoke up. "You should be able to crawl on your belly very nicely under that beam. Unless, of course, the floor in there is charged, too."

"Not . . . not that I know of."

"Well, you'll find out, won't you? Go ahead."

Under the threat of the d'Alembert guns, Rawling got down on her stomach and crawled forward into the room. She crept over the fallen door and then, with great trepidation, put a hand down on the floor. Nothing happened, so she crawled forward with more confidence toward the door at the far end of the room. Jules

162

and Yvette, seeing her go unharmed, got down and followed after her.

Rawling reached the other side and pushed the door open; the knob on that one, apparently, was not booby-trapped. As she entered the open corridor, she stood up and looked behind her. Jules and Yvette were still down on their stomachs, which gave her the perfect chance to escape. Without another instant's hesitation, she turned to the right and ran off as fast as she could. Jules fired his blaster at her, but she was out of the doorway long before the beam would have hit.

"Damn," he exclaimed as he pulled himself through the doorway. Rawling was already too far down the hall; she would have been out of his blaster range, and he didn't even try. "There goes our guide and passport."

"You'd better go after her," Yvette said, pulling herself out of the deadly room, too, and standing up. "She could rally her men and bring them down here after us."

"What about you?"

Yvette set her jaw. "I'm going after Garst," she said firmly. "He and I have an outstanding debt to settle."

Jules nodded. He knew that neither he nor any force in the Universe would come between herself and Garst now that she was again on the scent. "Smooth—but be careful which doors you open." Then he took off to the right after the fleeing security chief.

Yvette stood in the hallway for a moment, her mind racing in a coldly calculating manner. *Rawling would run in the direction away from Garst's office, to draw us off,* she reasoned. *His room must be to the left.* And she started out in the opposite direction from her brother.

The hallway made a turn to the right, and Yvette found herself in a corridor that led to a dead end a hundred meters away. On her right were five doors. One of them would have to be the correct one, but there was no way of guessing which. She would have to try all of them.

The first door was not boobytrapped, and showed a glimpse inside of a command center. Security Central, Yvette decided. There was no one there at present; Rawling must have deserted her post for some reason to serve on the front lines. Perhaps they were desperate for manpower. At any event, a quick skim showed Yvette that there was nothing in here to interest her. She continued on.

The second door turned out to be boobytrapped the same way the other room had been; when Yvette blew the door in, a blaster beam came slicing out, aimed at anyone standing in front of the door. She crawled under the beam and looked around inside the room, but it was empty.

The third door was free of traps, and led to a well-appointed private apartment. *This must be where Garst lives*, the agent thought as she padded quietly through the flat. She looked everywhere, but there was no sign of the apartment's inhabitant so she went outside to the hallway to try again.

As the next doorway fell before her blaster, she caught sight of Helena slumped in a chair against the far wall. She raced into the room with her gun drawn, ready to blast down anyone who moved.

Her passage across the threshold tripped an electric eye beam, which released a heavy deadfall from over her head. Any normal person would have been crushed under the weight of the massive block of metal as it came crashing down—but Yvette d'Alembert was not precisely a normal person. The gravitational pull on Sanctuary was approximately Earth normal, which meant that the deadfall dropped with an acceleration of one gee. Yvette came from a world where objects fell at three times that rate, and could react accordingly. She sensed the deadfall coming at her and leaped aside; the massive weight grazed her shoulder enough to wrench it and send pain all through her left side—but she was far from dead.

Yvette hit the floor, rolled, got to her knees and looked around the room. There was Garst, cowering in one corner, blaster in hand. He was pointing it at the spot where she'd fallen, but she was not there any more.

Hastily he tried to readjust his aim, but his reflexes were no match for hers. Yvette's blaster beam lashed out and found its intended mark—Garst's face. The archcriminal let out an abortive scream as the blaster burned almost instantly through his skull, searing skin, bone and brain tissue along its route.

Garst was dead almost immediately, but still Yvette did not stop firing. Slowly, meticulously, she ran her fiery beam up and down the length of Garst's body, charring it until the air inside the room reeked of burned human flesh. "That's for Dak," she muttered under her breath. "That's for a quarter of a million people, but mostly for Dak, you utter, complete bastard. I hate you!"

The process continued for some minutes, until all that was left of the criminal mastermind was a charred lump that was even unrecognizable as having been a human being. Finally, the anger drained from her body, Yvette took her finger off the trigger and lowered the gun. Her entire body was shaking, and it took a second to bring her eyes back into focus. Not until then did she remember the real purpose for her coming here, and she turned back to look at Helena.

The Head's daughter was unconscious. Her eyes were bloodshot, her pulse ragged and, when Yvette quickly rolled up the girl's sleeves, the veins were standing out grotesquely on the inside of Helena's arms. Yvette, with her specialized training, recognized those symptoms easily—the aftereffects of a dose of nitrobarb.

It would be risky moving Helena at all while she was suffering from this condition. Grimly, Yvette pulled up a chair beside Helena's and waited for Jules to arrive.

CHAPTER 13

Explosive Results

When Rawling went running down the hallway, she knew she'd be in for the race of her life. DesPlainians were well noted for their speed, and one or both of her captors would be after her in a matter of seconds. They dared not let her run loose.

The best advantage she had was that she knew the layout of this complex and they did not. She was unarmed at the moment and there weren't any more of the boobytrapped rooms in this direction, but perhaps she would be able to find one of her guards who was not busy fighting the mob upstairs. Failing that, she would have to get to the armory and find a new weapon. She knew that her first judo throw of that one agent had been a fluke, and she had no desire to test her skills further in hand-to-hand fighting with an obviously accomplished professional. Besides, *he* had a gun and would not hesitate to use it.

She arrived at the door to the armory, but it was locked. She had a key, but it was buried deep in one of her pockets and she could not afford the precious seconds it would take to dig it out. Already she thought she could hear a set of footsteps racing down the corridors after her. After pausing barely long enough to take a deep breath, she ran on.

Turning a corner rapidly, she ran full tilt into another

heavy-grav male, dressed as a dandy complete with cape, hat and rose. They were both knocked to the ground by the surprise impact but Rawling, her reflexes aided by the surges of adrenalin being pumped through her bloodstream, recovered her wits a fraction of a second before the man.

She lashed out with her foot, and the kick caught Pias Bavol just under the jaw. His head snapped backward against the floor, and his body went limp. The security chief scrambled to her feet and picked up the blaster the other had been carrying. She was armed now, too—a fact unknown to her pursuer. She could use that to her advantage. Within seconds he would come racing around that same corner after her. He would be holding his blaster at the ready but, even with his quick instincts, he would not be able to fire before she could.

She set the beam of her captured gun on its broadest width, so that she could hardly miss hitting something. The initial hit would be at a less-than-deadly intensity, but it would so wound her pursuer that she would have the time to finish him off. Backing into a doorway, she focused every iota of her attention on the mouth of the corridor and waited.

Jules was running as silently as he could, but even so his footsteps echoed hollowly down the otherwise empty halls. Rawling could estimate his approach with reasonable precision, while he had no way of knowing she was lying in ambush for him. As he came around the corner, he instantly spotted her standing in front of him, her blaster up and ready to shoot. He pointed his own gun, but he knew it would not be in time. Rawling had gotten the drop on him.

Then, before either of those two could fire, a buzzing sound emanated from the floor of the corridor. So intent had Rawling been on watching for Jules's appearance that she had not bothered to watch the slow, careful motions of her supposedly disarmed and unconscious victim of a few moments before. The security chief fell helplessly to the ground.

As Jules allowed himself to bounce off the wall to slow his terrific momentum, Pias Bavol got slowly to his feet. In his right hand was a ministunner; his left hand was busy stroking his bruised jaw tenderly. "She had quite a kick, that lady. I presume she was no friend of yours."

Jules bent his head a moment and took some deep breaths. "No. And that's the second time tonight you've saved my life."

Pias dismissed that with a gallant wave of his hand. "My pleasure. I'm just glad my pet dog once taught me how to play dead—it's a trick that really comes in handy."

"Where did you find that thing?" Jules asked, pointing at the ministunner. He knew such weaponry was not generally available here on Sanctuary.

"From here." The Newforester picked up his hat and, upon close inspection, Jules could see that there was a small holster right behind the flower's blossom. The holster was unnoticeable unless one knew precisely where to look. "Every rose must have its thorn," Pias continued blithely as he tucked the weapon away once more.

"You're not as helpless as you appear at first glance," Jules commented. The praise came grudgingly from him.

"Thank you. Given a choice, I would prefer to have my enemies underestimate me. Much safer that way. Where's your sister?"

"She went the other way, looking for our friend." He looked down at Rawling's unconscious form. "How long will she be out?"

169

"The maximum setting for a mini like mine is five, which is what I gave her. She should be out for six hours."

"Plenty of time, then," Jules nodded. "We can leave her here for now. Let's go back and see if Yv . . . Yarmilla needs my help."

They started back at a fast jog in the direction from which Jules had come. Their pace gave them a little more time to look at the scenery along the way. As they ran, Jules suddenly came to a halt outside the door marked "Armory." "This looks interesting," he said. "Let's have a look for a second."

The door was locked, but the two men did not let that stop them. Focusing both their blasters on the door, they burned out the locking device and were able to push the massive portal inward.

Inside the room they found enough weapons to supply a small army. There were blasters of varying powers, from the lightweight hand models all the way up to the big heavy duty ones mounted on mobile tripods. There were dozens of large boxes marked "Explosives," along with all the peripheral detonation equipment. There were, it seemed, several hundred suits of battle armor, both for land-based use and for space application. Looking over the array of destructive capacity, Pias gave a low whistle. "They wanted to be ready for anything, didn't they?"

"There's enough equipment here to repel any major attack," Jules confirmed. "Or to launch an attack of their own. They could probably take a small agricultural planet with this gear and a staff of well-trained people, if they timed their assault properly."

He ushered Pias out of the room again. "Let's go find my sister before we decide what to make of all that. I have a hunch it may come in handy."

The two men continued down the hallway to the spot

where Jules and Yvette had split up. They then followed the path in the other direction, retracing Yvette's steps. They went under the blaster beam that continued firing out of the one boobytrapped door and came to the door that Yvette had intentionally left open. Jules peeked in cautiously. His sister was watching the doorway, blaster in hand and looking very relieved that it was he who had entered rather than some guards. Beside Yvette, looking pale and lifeless, Helena's body was slumped in her chair.

"Is she all right?" Jules asked quickly.

"Nitrobarb." That one word summed up the situation. After a second, Yvette added, "I killed Garst. There's no doubt about it, this time." Her voice sounded very tired and very far away.

"Good." For a moment, Jules didn't know what else to say. Pias entered the room behind him, and Yvette's expression picked up a little. Jules, taking heart from the change, said, "What can we do? Can she be moved?"

"Not readily," Yvette replied. She'd had more formal training than her brother in the effects of nitrobarb. "Her metabolism is in a precarious balance right now. Any sudden changes in her condition could tip that balance the wrong way."

"How long do we have to wait?"

"Ten, twenty hours, depending on how long she's already been in coma. It's hard to tell, exactly."

"I'm a newcomer to all this, I admit," Pias Bavol spoke up, "but I honestly don't think we can afford to wait that long. The rioters and guards are fighting it out upstairs right now, which is fine for us—but that won't continue much longer. One side or the other will emerge victorious, and the winner will be coming down here. Whichever side that is, I don't want to be around when it happens."

171

"He's right," Jules sighed. "Whether it's safe or not, we'll have to move her out of here."

"But where?" Yvette asked. "We can't go carrying her out the way we came in—there are too many guards, too many obstacles. We barely made it in here on our own; we'd never get out alive carrying an essentially dead weight."

"We may not have to," Pias said. "I suspect there's another, more private way out of here."

Jules clapped his hands together at the Newforester's revelation. "Of course! Garst came from Vesa, a world of underground tunnels. His mentality was that of a crafty burrowing animal—and most burrowing animals always leave themselves a back door in case of attack."

Pias nodded. "My Gypsy ancestors back on Earth were always conscious of the need to keep an escape route open. You never could tell when one would be needed." He stroked his chin thoughtfully. "But where would there be on this planet to escape to? Not back into the city, there would be too much chance of being spotted there. Possibly an underground retreat outside the city where he had enough supplies stored to last out a search."

Yvette shook her head. "I don't think so," she said, entering into the speculation game. "Garst wasn't one to wait out trouble; we've already seen that when something goes wrong he tries to get as far from the scene as he possibly can—and he doesn't stop running until he's clear across the Galaxy."

"A ship," Jules said. "He'd have to have a ship of his own, all ready to take off in case of trouble. And he'd have his own private tunnel to it, because in an emergency he couldn't count on getting to the spaceport by the normal route. Let's search this room thoroughly; I'm willing to bet we can find that tunnel."

With the three of them looking, they were able to

172

cover the room quite thoroughly. They found nothing the first time through, but on their second, closer inspection Jules found a hidden drawer. Pulling it out, he discovered several dozen videotape reels, bookreels and other records.

"Garst was always a thorough bookkeeper," Yvette commented. "His records on Vesa were quite helpful. I suggest we take those with us when we go; I know someone who'll be interested in seeing what's on them."

Jules nodded and continued searching.

On their third time around the chamber, Yvette found what they were after. Her hand pressed firmly over a row of seemingly decorative studs, and suddenly a portion of one wall slid away, revealing a narrow corridor that did indeed lead out in the direction of the spaceport. "Let's get going," Pias said.

"It's not quite that simple," Jules told him. "There are things that have to be planned first."

"What, for instance?"

"For instance," Yvette answered his question, "as soon as we get out into space, we'll take some astrogational measurements and find out exactly where this place is. Then we intend to call a friend of ours and have reinforcements sent in to shut Sanctuary down."

"That's a good idea," Pias nodded.

"But," the female d'Alembert continued, "as soon as the rioting calms down out there, some people may realize what will be happening. They'll try to escape on some of the ships that are sitting out there on the spaceport field right now. If we could think of some way to destroy all those ships, the police could make a clean sweep when they come in here."

"I know how to do it, too," Jules added. "They've got an armory stockpiled with plenty of explosives and weapons—more than we'll need."

"*Khorosho,*" Yvette said. "I'll carry our sleeping

173

beauty out to the ship while you go back and get the explosives. You'd better hurry, too—it'll be morning soon, which will make the job that much harder."

The two men returned to the armory immediately. Pias admitted that he knew very little about the exotic weaponry there, so Jules was left with the task of composing their shopping list. He chose another blaster each for the three of them and two armloads of explosives. Then he rigged up some more explosives on a timed fuse within the armory itself. "This is to destroy their cache so they won't be able to mount much resistance when the good guys show up," Jules explained to the puzzled Newforester.

Pias nodded slowly. There were obviously a great many more details to this business than he himself would ever have imagined.

Then, carrying their loads of explosives, the two men raced back to Garst's main office and down the secret tunnel to the ship, where they found Yvette and the unconscious Helena waiting for them. "It's a simple craft," Yvette told them, "but it's likely to be cramped—it's only a two-seater. Garst obviously wasn't planning to save too many people besides himself."

They divided up the explosives, and the d'Alemberts gave their new friend a brief but thorough course in demolitions. When they were through, they made him repeat the instructions back to them twice to make sure he knew what he was doing. Then the trio left Helena alone in Garst's getaway ship and went out to wreak their destruction.

There were ninety-six ships currently standing out on the port field, and only one shift of ten guards to watch over them. Consequently, the three dark figures were able to move stealthily at will through the early morning darkness and attach their explosive devices unseen to the bottoms of the vessels. It took better than two hours to complete the mission, and then they were to rendezvous back at Garst's ship.

Jules and Yvette arrived back before Pias. They had been able to work faster because they were more familiar with the gear and, even though they had given him a smaller share of the work, they'd finished before he had. Jules slipped into the pilot's chair and began giving the ship a preflight checkout while Yvette stood in the hatchway and looked out over the field, hoping to see some sign of the Newforester.

There was a flash and a loud roar from the headquarters complex over at one side of the spaceport field. "There goes the armory," Jules commented without looking up from his control board. "The rest of the fireworks should be starting any time now."

"I wish he'd get back," Yvette muttered under her breath.

The guards at the spaceport were quite perplexed about the explosion at headquarters, and were not quite sure how to react to it. A couple of minutes later, however, a freighter at the end of the field farthest from Garst's ship also blew up, scattering fragments for a hundred meters around. That situation was clearly listed in their instructions—sabotage. Within seconds of that explosion, floodlights came on all over the port, illuminating all but the remotest corners of the field.

There, standing in open territory, was Pias Bavol. He had apparently finished with his final ship and was on his way back when the lights had caught him in an exposed position. He was nearly three hundred meters away, and was the only figure out in the middle of the field. The guards could not help but spot him.

"Pias!" Yvette exclaimed involuntarily, even though she knew he was too far away to hear her.

Jules was beside her in an instant, looking the situation over. It took only a fraction of a second to see what

175

had happened and what needed to be done. "You stay here with Helena," he said. "You're better trained to help her. I'll go out and get him." And, before she could object, he was out the hatch and racing down the ladder as fast as he could move.

Two more explosions shook the ground as a pair of ships blew up almost simultaneously. Yvette could only stand helplessly in the hatchway as she watched the two men she loved so dearly running toward one another. There were more explosions; once they started, they seemed to go in strings like firecrackers.

The guards were totally confused by the chaos around them, but they knew that, if they couldn't stop the sabotage, they could at least try to stop the saboteurs. The figures of Jules and Pias were entirely too conspicuous on the otherwise deserted field, giving the sentries an excellent opportunity for target practice.

Jules was only fifty meters away from Pias when the latter fell forward after a blaster beam clipped his calf. Yvette gasped, and saw her brother redouble his efforts to reach the Newforester before the guard could reaim his weapon. Pias lay motionless on the ground, and Yvette's heart felt as though it had stopped completely. *Does every man I love have to die because of Garst's machinations?* she thought desperately. *It isn't fair . . . it just isn't fair!*

Then Jules was beside Pias and dragging the other man to a position of temporary safety behind a ship that wasn't scheduled to blow up for another couple of minutes. Pias seemed conscious, and he and Jules conferred for a moment on the state of the leg. Jules helped the Newforester to his feet, and they tested to see whether the injured limb could support Pias's full body weight. Pias was nodding, indicating he thought he could make it on his own.

Jules let the other go ahead of him. Pias tried manfully to run, but the wound in his leg turned his gait into an off-balance shamble. Jules followed behind, gun drawn and ready to pick off any guard who might attempt to snipe at the man who had twice that evening saved his life.

Every few seconds, it seemed, the ground was rocked by another explosion. Several more fires had broken out around the area, but all the firefighting equipment was being used in the city and there was nothing the guards could do to extinguish the blazes. The thick black smoke that rapidly filled the morning air helped cover Jules and Pias as they made their agonizing way back to the ship.

The two men at last reached the base of the ladder and started to climb up. Yvette took her eyes off them now and started watching the field. This would be the moment of maximum exposure, when the men would be helpless and perfect targets against the smooth metal hull of the ship. Yvette scrutinized the field, her gaze tracking back and forth like a human radar. No one was going to kill her men if she had anything to say in the matter.

A motion to the left caught her eye, and Yvette fired instinctively. The guard who was about to shoot at the climbing figures was just at the limit of Yvette's range, and her blaster bolt did not kill him, even though it struck dead center. The beam did, however, produce enough of a heat jolt that it knocked the man backwards off his feet. It would take him a couple of minutes to recover from that blow—and by the time he did, Jules and Pias had made it inside the hatch. Yvette took the Newforester by the arm and led him gently into the control cabin while Jules shut the hatch behind them and dogged it airtight.

"I'm going to need the acceleration couch to pilot this ship," Jules said as he passed by his two conscious

177

comrades to get to the controls. "Girl Friday will need the other to protect her as much as possible from the effects of the acceleration. That doesn't leave much space for you."

"How fast will you be taking off?" Pias asked. Yvette had already gotten the ship's small first aid kit and was bandaging his leg. The blaster had taken a small chunk out of the skin on his left thigh, but the wound was more painful than serious.

"No more than three gees," Yvette advised her brother. "Our other patient certainly couldn't take more than that. As it is, we're having to depend awfully heavily on the fact that she's young and in perfect health. Every time something new happens to her, it reduces the chance of her survival still further."

"All right then," Jules agreed. "Nice and slow."

"In that case," Pias said, "Yarmilla and I can lie side by side on the back wall. At three gees, it won't be any worse than lying on the ground back home."

Jules nodded and continued to set the controls, while outside on the field the other ships continued to explode around them. After five minutes, he announced he was ready, and Yvette and Pias braced themselves.

There was a dull whine as the ship's engines sprang to life under Jules's deft touch. The whine progressed to a roar, and then suddenly they felt themselves pressed downward by the upward thrust of the ship's acceleration. The pull of three gees was far from painful; in fact, it produced a feeling of comfort the three of them had been missing for quite some time.

Slowly, then, the little ship lifted itself into the skies. The three adventurers had done the seemingly impossible—they had come to Sanctuary, accomplished their respective tasks—and escaped alive to tell the tale.

CHAPTER 14

The Marquis of Newforest

The acceleration seemed to go on forever; because they were lifting off the world at such a comparatively gentle pace, it took them a longer time to establish their preliminary orbit. But eventually they made it, and Jules shut off the drive. Instantly they felt the change from three gees to none and, even though Jules had warned them when to expect it, it still came as a shock to their systems.

Yvette's first concern was for Helena. The Head's daughter was looking extremely pale as Yvette swam hastily toward her and felt at her throat for a pulse. "Ragged, but there," she sighed after a moment. "Maybe she'll make it yet."

Jules's efforts did not cease once they were safely in space, however. He was taking sightings on various stars to determine exactly what octant of the Galaxy they were in and what the coordinates of this star system were. It took him better than half an hour just to make the basic measurements, and then another hour to run his calculations through the shipboard computer. But eventually he did discover their exact whereabouts, and was able from that point to send out a subcom call to the Head back on Earth.

As he started to put the call through, he gave a slight nod to his sister, who found a pretext to have Pias join her belowdeck in the tiny galley. Although the New-

179

forester had proven to be a good ally, they could not risk revealing the Head's identity to someone about whom they still knew so little.

Garst's subcom did not have a Service scrambler as did the d'Alembert vessel, so Jules intentionally left the visual circuits off, both for transmitting and receiving. When the Head's voice came over the speaker, Jules spoke slowly, encoding his message in one of SOTE's top codes as he went along. The first thing he mentioned was that they had gotten Helena out, but that she had been given nitrobarb and was not yet past the danger point. He reported that Garst had been the person running the operation on Sanctuary, and probably the person who had administered the nitrobarb and learned all of Helena's secrets. But Garst was now quite definitely dead, and anything he learned had died with him—unless, Jules added significantly, he had passed the information along to someone else before the d'Alemberts had reached him. The Head listened to that speculation somberly, but did not interrupt Jules's report.

Jules gave the coordinates for Sanctuary's star system and requested that several naval vessels be detailed to pick up the criminals they would find down on the planet's surface. He had destroyed most or all of the ships on the spaceport field, Jules said, but new ships were arriving there every day and might be able to take some of the "clients" away before the Imperial Navy could arrive.

The Head took a moment to check the position of naval ships in that Sector, and then assured his agent that a Navy vessel could reach Sanctuary in at most two and a half days. In the meantime, he would also issue orders to have the entire region around Sanctuary cordoned off, so that all ships coming out of that particular volume of space would be thoroughly searched. A handful of lucky crooks might elude the blockade, but the vast majority would be captured and turned over to the appropriate authorities.

Jules mentioned their newfound friend, Pias Bavol, and requested a security check on him. There was silence on the other end for a moment, and then the Head replied, "I don't think that will be necessary."

"Why not, sir?"

"The Bavols have already been thoroughly investigated for their loyalty as a matter of routine. Pias is the eldest child of the Duke of Newforest, which makes him a marquis and heir to the entire planet. Newforesters were suspect when they were first brought into the Empire fifty years ago, but they've proven their loyalty since then. Unless you have some special reason to doubt him, I'd give him a tentative smooth rating."

Jules was stunned. Pias had given them no indication that he was of the nobility; but then, they had hidden the same fact from him. Their father, Etienne d'Alembert, was Duke of DesPlaines, though it was their older brother Robert who would inherit the title. Jules and Yvette merely had the formal rank of Lord and Lady—a rank they seldom had occasion to use.

Jules assured his boss that they would head for Earth at all possible speed. He wasn't sure exactly how fast Garst's ship was capable of traveling, but he estimated the flight time between seven and ten days. And, of course, he would subcom a message the instant they knew whether Helena would survive the nitrobarb. The Head thanked him for his kindness and concern, and the two broke the connection. Then Jules made the necessary preparations for dropping the ship into subspace.

Yvette was equally surprised when she learned of Pias's rank. When the two of them confronted him about it, he just looked sheepish and admitted that he was indeed the Marquis of Newforest.

"Why didn't you tell us this before?" Yvette asked.

"It didn't seem germane to the situation," Pias answered with a shrug.

Helena hovered on the brink of death for hours. Shortly after they entered subspace, the girl broke out in a deep sweat. Her body was drenched in perspiration, and her clothes clung to her like a second skin. All three of the others took turns sponging her off with damp pieces of cloth. At one point her temperature hovered close to forty celsius, and her friends began to despair.

Several hours later, she passed into a state of hallucinations. She would scream and shriek, mostly in gibberish with only a few words recognizable. She thrashed around so violently that it took all of Jules's Des-Plainian strength to hold her and prevent her from hurting herself. In freefall, the situation was even worse than it would have been under gravity conditions.

When those fits passed, Helena was suddenly struck with fierce chills. They wrapped her in the only two blankets they could find aboard the ship, and Jules again held her, this time to lend his body heat as well as his strength. Finally the bout of chills passed, too, and Helena floated in the control room, her entire body pale, her chest barely moving to indicate she was breathing. "We'll know soon," Yvette said—and her voice was far from confident.

Jules was standing watch over their patient when her eyelids began flickering weakly. He bent over her as one eyelid pried open for a second before closing again. Instantly, Jules called for his sister, and Yvette was at his side in a moment.

Helena's eyelids flickered some more before she was finally able to open both eyes and stare, uncomprehendingly at first, at the faces of her two close friends. Yvette had deliberately lowered the room lighting so that the sudden glare would not be too blinding.

"How do you feel?" Jules asked compassionately.

Helena's mind was confused for a moment, and her thoughts traveled in random paths. Then, with a rush, all the memories came flying back at her—the attempted escape, the fighting at the spaceport, the capture, and then her interrogation by Garst up to the point where he injected her with the nitrobarb. She had obviously pulled through and her friends were with her—and she was in freefall. But more than that, she could not guess.

"Very dizzy, very weak and very confused," she replied truthfully. "It's good to see both of you, though. I never thought I'd see anything again." Then, as Pias moved into her line of sight, she suddenly became very suspicious. "Who's he?" she asked.

Carefully, Jules and Yvette gave her a step by step account of the events following Helena's capture at the spaceport. The care was taken, not for Helena's benefit, but for Pias's; he might be a loyal subject of the Emperor, but even so they did not go about blurting out classified information to any loyal citizen unless he had the need to know. Helena realized the ground rules and read their story between the lines.

While Jules was putting through another subcom call to the Head to let him know his daughter was out of danger, Yvette shooed Pias out of the room and asked Helena, "Well, what do you think of field work now?"

Helena smiled ruefully. "You were right. I think I've had enough of it to last me the rest of my life. There are advantages to sitting safely behind a desk and letting you take the risks."

"Everybody does what he can do best," Yvette nodded. "Your paperwork is no less essential than our field duties. Our job only *looks* more glamorous."

The trip back to Earth took a total of eight days in the cramped quarters of Garst's ship. During that time, there was little to do except for all of them to get better acquainted. Helena was introduced to Marquis Pias, though Jules and Yvette refrained from giving Helena's name. Unfortunately, none of the three SOTE people could really talk about themselves very much, which left much of the conversational burden on Pias's shoulders. He was a glib talker, though, and if he minded their secretiveness he didn't let it show. By the time they reached Earth, even Jules had to admit his initial impression of the Newforester had been mistaken, and that the man was really a nice guy, after all. Yvette gave him a smug smile and said nothing. It was obvious that her own feelings toward the man were deepening as well.

When they landed at the Canaveral Spaceport they were greeted by an ambulance, which whisked Helena off to a hospital despite her assurances that she'd been out of her coma for a week and was feeling almost back to normal. Jules, Yvette and Pias left the ship anonymously and checked into one of the swanker nearby hotels. As soon as the Head was satisfied that they'd left the ship, he had it confiscated and Garst's records were seized and analyzed.

Two uneventful days passed for Jules and Yvette. They were beginning to wonder whether they'd been forgotten when they received orders to appear at the Ambassador Suite on the top floor of their hotel that night for a very private meeting. There was little doubt in their minds about the general nature of that rendezvous.

Grand Duke Zander von Wilmenhorst himself opened the doors for them and ushered them inside the suite. Duchess Helena was lying stretched out on one long sofa; she started to get to her feet when the others entered, but they all insisted that she stay just where she was. Her face was still quite pale, though some color was slowly beginning to creep back into her cheeks.

"First off," the Head said after all the hellos had been exchanged, "I'd like to express my personal thanks for all the two of you have done on this assignment. You brought my daughter back safely; I don't know of anyone else who could have done as good a job under the circumstances."

"We did have some help," Yvette pointed out.

"Yes, I intend to discuss your friend the Marquis later. Right now, please accept the gratitude of a loving father for the safe return of his daughter."

"We were happy to do it," Jules replied. "Helena's our friend, too."

"Now to speak as your boss," the Head went on, shifting his tone of voice to a more professional level. "I'd like to say I'm gratified with the work you've done for me—even though it points the way to still more work that needs to be done. The conspiracy we're facing is an enormous one; it may even be bigger than Banion's network."

The d'Alemberts exchanged startled glances. The conspiracy masterminded by Banion the Bastard had spanned more than three quarters of the Empire, had infiltrated some of the highest levels of the Service itself, and had been nearly fifty years in the planning. Could *anything* be bigger than that?

"How much of Garst's records did you read over?" the Head continued.

"Not much," Yvette admitted. "Most of it was in the form of tapes, and we simply didn't have the equipment aboard ship to play them back. Then too, with Pias there we were reluctant to let too much out of the bag."

"Commendable," the Head nodded. "But I've been studying what you brought back and, frankly, it scares me silly. Particularly one tape.

"As you know, we first became aware of a deep-set conspiracy when your cousin Luise learned from the late Dr. Rustin about the other robots he'd made. The information you obtained on Mellisande confirmed that, and added another piece—Lady A. She seemed to be a focal point for the activities, a very high official in that conspiracy. Well, she turned up again in Garst's office—unfortunately, on the same day Helena arrived. Garst very conveniently kept taped records of most of the conversations that occurred there. Let me play that particular tape for you."

The Head went over to the videorecorder he'd set up in one corner of the room and pressed a button. The d'Alemberts sat silently—and in shock—as they watched and listened to the conversation. They saw Lady A for the first time and heard her voice as she identified Zander von Wilmenhorst as Head of the Service, and Helena as his chief assistant. They listened to her claim that she and her organization knew most of what went on in SOTE, and her implied statement that she was working toward the overthrow of the Empire. When the tape was over, they sat, stunned, for several seconds.

"I've shown that tape to Bill," the Head said quietly, "and his reaction was much the same as yours." The reference could be to only one person—His Imperial Majesty William Stanley, tenth of his royal line, supreme ruler of the Empire of Earth. "I offered him my resignation, on the grounds that the knowledge of my identity would limit my effectiveness. He rejected that out of hand, saying that he still thought I was the best man for the job and that I should be able to handle any contingency."

"I agree with him, sir," Jules said. "I have full confidence in you. But that tape *is* dismaying."

"Thank you. You have a talent, though, for understatement. That tape is devastating. We thought we'd plugged all the leaks in our office after the Banion affair, and yet we seem to be more porous than ever. I'd stake my life on the people we have working under us, yet there continues to be a leak."

"Could one of our trustworthy people have been replaced by one of Dr. Rustin's robots?" Yvette suggested.

Their boss shook his head. "No, that was one of the first things that occurred to me, too. But as soon as we learned about the existence of those robots we X-rayed all our personnel and they checked out as human. We did it again yesterday after I saw that tape, with the same results. There are no robot infiltrators in our top echelons. Whatever the real answer is, it's a lot more complex than that. Did either of you recognize that woman?"

Both Jules and Yvette had to admit that they'd never seen her before.

"Neither have I," the Head sighed. "Yet she must operate largely on Earth, since this is the seat of government; she'd have to stay close if she wanted to keep her finger on SOTE's pulse. Also, her clothes were in the latest Court fashion, indicating she is a person of some means or rank. But that is the only real clue we have."

"What do you intend to do then, sir?" Jules asked.

"Espionage is a game of secrets within secrets. It's not merely a matter of finding out what the other side knows; you also have to keep them guessing about how

187

much *you* know. At the moment, there are only five people in the Galaxy who know we've seen that tape—the four of us in this room and Bill. Even Irene and Edna haven't been informed of it, nor will they be. The two of you are not to make any mention of it to anyone, not even your relatives. There will be no record of its existence anywhere; as far as the Service is officially concerned, the tapes found in Garst's office were inconsequential records, nothing more. If the enemy knows that the tape exists at all, they will have no way of knowing we've seen it. That will give us some slight advantage. *Bozhe* knows, we need it."

"What about our identities?" Jules asked. "One of our major assets has always been that no one else in the Service has been aware of the role the Circus plays. Only a few people in SOTE—like Marask Kantana, for instance—have ever seen our faces, and they don't know the whole truth. Does the enemy know about that now, too?"

Here Helena blushed fiercely. "I feel so embarrassed about that. There's a tape of Garst interrogating me, and I told him everything about you and the Circus."

"You couldn't help it," Yvette soothed. "You were under nitrobarb. You were lucky to live."

"From the way Garst was questioning her," Helena's father went on, "it was obvious that the information was new and stunning to him. If Lady A and her friends know, they didn't let him in on the secret. And he never told them, either, for some reason. The Navy personnel who took over Sanctuary report that the subcom was not used between the time Garst questioned Helena and the time you killed him. Whatever he knew died with him.

"Of course, we have no way of knowing whether Lady A is aware of you through her other sources—but something, call it intuition, makes me doubt that very

188

much. I don't think she'd be quite so confident if she did, and I think she would have ordered Garst to kill Helena immediately, because she'd have known I'd send you in after her. She may be aware of your code names—everyone in the Service is—but she still doesn't know your capabilities. I intend to keep it that way. Security about your identities will be tighter than ever.

"And speaking of that brings us to the subject of Pias Bavol. I understand, Yvette my dear, that you are quite taken with the man."

"He asked me yesterday morning to become engaged to him," Yvette said quietly. "I told him I'd need some time to think about it."

"Meaning that you wanted to talk it over with me," the Head smiled. "That's very wise of you. Tell me, how do you feel about him?"

"I love him very much," the female d'Alembert said without an instant's hesitation. "I'd love to marry him. But I have a duty to the Service, and I can't allow any conflict there. If you feel he'd be a security risk, I'll have to turn him down."

"What do you think of him, Jules?"

"I didn't like him at first," the other agent admitted. "He was too flashy, too talky and acted in too suspicious a manner. But as the going got tougher, so did he. I can't entirely condone what he did to Carnery—but I can't say I wouldn't do the same thing if someone were to butcher Vonnie."

"If he were to marry Yvette, we'd have to bring him into the network and give him agent training. How do you think he'd do?"

"Initially, I wouldn't have thought very much of his chances. But he tracked his man for two years without having any formal training at all. He got to Sanctuary and completed his mission without help from anyone else; he might even have been able to get away without anyone's help if our paths hadn't crossed so violently. If, as you say, his loyalty is above question then yes, I'd sponsor him through the training academy."

Yvette wanted to lean over and kiss her brother, but restrained her enthusiasm.

The Head looked at Yvette. "You realize he'll have to be told virtually everything. About your identities, about your background, about the Circus—the whole works. Your family will want to meet him before they give their approval, though I don't think Etienne would hold back on such a marriage. Bavol will have to know everything except the matter of the Garst tape; that I intend to keep secret among the five who already know it. I'll rely on your judgment—do you trust the Marquis that much? Your lives may depend on the answer."

"He's already saved my life once, and Jules's twice," Yvette replied. "And both times he didn't have to. He could have let us die and didn't. Yes, I'd trust him again in a second." And Jules gave a quiet nod of agreement.

"*Khorosho*," said the Head with a smile. "If my two best agents are willing to put their lives in this man's hands, I can do no less. He is not to know my identity, of course—though if he ever sees Helena at a public function he'll probably guess. I'll leave it to you to break the news to him, and I'll see that he's admitted to the Service Academy."

There were tears of happiness in Yvette's eyes as her boss spoke. Helena got up off her couch and came over to give her friend a sisterly kiss on the cheek and the two women began talking over the details of the marriage—whether it would be before or after Pias's training, what kind of ceremony it would be, and so forth.

Zander von Wilmenhorst watched them with mixed emotions. His mind was considering a wedding, too, but one that few people yet knew about. The announcement would soon be made that Crown Princess Edna would be marrying the man of her choice, a man named Choyen Liu. With her being the only child of the Emperor, Edna's wedding would command the attention of the entire Galaxy—and, he presumed, the attention of Lady A and her mob as well. Something would be afoot, he was sure of that, though what it would be he couldn't even begin to guess right now. He would be responsible for security, and nothing could be allowed to jeopardize the safety of the Princess and the Succession.

He pushed those thoughts to the back of his mind as he focused his attention once more on his two top agents, Jules and Yvette d'Alembert. *They've earned a brief vacation,* he told himself. *I can afford to give them a little rest before they have to save the Galaxy again.*